The Week of the Horse

The
WEEK
of the
HORSE

Jocelyn Reekie

DISCARD

RAINCOAST BOOKS

Vancouver

Raincoast Books acknowledges the ongoing financial support of the Government of Canada through The Canada Council for the Arts and the Book Publishing Industry Development Program (BPIDP); and the Government of British Columbia through the BC Arts Council.

Editor: Lynn Henry
Cover artwork: Julia Bell
Cover and text design: Val Speidel

NATIONAL LIBRARY OF CANADA CATALOGUING IN PUBLICATION:

Reekie, Jocelyn, 1947-
    The week of the horse / Jocelyn Reekie.

ISBN 1-55192-655-5

    1. Horses--Juvenile fiction. I. Title.

PS8585.E422W43 2004   jC813'.6   C2003-906947-8

LIBRARY OF CONGRESS CONTROL NUMBER: 2004090628

Raincoast Books   *In the United States:*
9050 Shaughnessy Street   Publishers Group West
Vancouver, British Columbia   1700 Fourth Street
Canada, V6P 6E5   Berkeley, California
www.raincoast.com   94710

Printed in Canada by Webcom
10 9 8 7 6 5 4 3 2 1

When I was a kid I was desperate for a horse. The summer I was thirteen I used babysitting money to rent a pony. When I told my mother what I'd done she didn't believe it, and so I brought the horse into our cottage kitchen to show her it was true. I kept the poor animal in a greenhouse for four days before he ran back to Flett's Farm. Thanks to Mr. Flett for his understanding and forgiveness. Years later, my second youngest sister, Jane, saved up and bought a horse she had trouble keeping and my husband's younger sister, Cindy, won a Shetland pony. That pony, too, kept running home.

This book is dedicated to dreams: to Cindy and Frisky, Jane and Dandy, and to the newest generation of dreamers —Haley, Kerry, Gaylan, Jaden and MJ — with much love.

— Contents —

One	1
Two	9
Three	18
Four	25
Five	37
Six	43
Seven	52
Eight	59
Nine	77
Ten	88
Eleven	92
Twelve	101
Thirteen	104
Fourteen	121
Fifteen	128
Sixteen	137

— One —

welve-year-old Paulie stood under Duke's long neck, leaning her back against his chest. In her left hand she held a piece of binder twine. Her right hand slid up the horse's cheek to the top of his head. She pulled his right ear, stroked it; then pressed her fingers against his poll. Duke's head came lower over her shoulder. His big lips twitched. He reached even lower and with his lips cleanly plucked a carrot from Paulie's jacket pocket, jerked his head upward, and tried to run. But he was too late. Paulie held fast to the ends of the twine she had slipped over his neck. "Haw," she laughed as she moved beside him. "That's twice this week this trick has worked. You're slowing down, boy." Her hands deftly looped and threaded the twine over his nose and behind his ears, fashioning a makeshift halter.

Duke snorted and soggy pieces of carrot spattered over Paulie's face and clothes. "Ew!" she complained. She pulled his lips apart. His teeth were angled like the jutting visor of old English armour. She whistled. "Look at those clackers. No edges left at all. I think we're gonna have to take you to a dentist and get you a set of false ones. Boy, think how big they'd have to be. A set of teeth like that'd be great for Halloween. By the way, did you know your teeth are extremely yellow? You ought to brush them more. Here, have another carrot." She pulled another from her pocket and broke it into pieces she allowed him to lip from the palm of her hand.

When he had taken the last piece, she led him to a low spot in the field and put him below her while she stood on the rim. Duke's eyelids slid to half-mast. Paulie caught a handful of his mane and jumped, but she wasn't fast enough. As she jumped Duke took one step sideways and his would-be rider found herself hanging down his side instead of sitting on his back.

She giggled helplessly. "All right," she gasped as she struggled to claw herself upright, "that's one for you." She was too busy to see the man who was running across the field toward them, but she heard him shout.

"Hey! Get away from that horse!"

At the sound, Duke crow-hopped violently sideways and Paulie, who was not quite upright yet, hit the ground hard. The man continued to run and Duke galloped away.

"Now look what you've done," the man scolded, offering his hand to Paulie. "Going and falling off and hurting yourself."

She bounced to her feet without his help and stood facing him, huffing. "What I've done! You're the one who spooked him! I wasn't falling off; I was getting on. It's a game we play."

"Well, you won't be playing games with that horse any more. We're about to load him up. You'd better run along home."

Surprise squashed Paulie's anger. "Bob didn't tell me Duke was going anywhere," she said. "Duke's a stable horse and I have permission to ride him anytime I want. Where's he going?"

"Stable's coming down. All the horses are going to auction. We're going to start loadin' any minute, so like I said you'd better head home now. Hey!" he yelled as Paulie ran for the fence and slipped between two rails. "Come back here."

Paulie raced across the parking lot, through the big end-doors of the riding arena, ran its length to another door, barrelled through that and ran across a grassy area that separated the arena from the main barn. She saw the one-ton truck backed up under the loft opening at the far end. As she ran toward that end, a bale of hay fell from the loft into the truck bed. She tore down the aisle until she came to a ladder that led up to the loft. Bob didn't see her until her head and shoulders appeared through the trap-door hole. "Hi, Brat," he said as he continued to throw bales into the truck below.

Paulie scrambled upward through the hole. "What's going on around here?" she demanded. "Some guy came racing and yelling across the field and spooked Duke so he dumped me and then this guy tells me the horses are going to the auction. He said the stable is going to be torn down."

"That's right," Bob answered. "I was going to tell you about it when you'd finished the stalls this morning but you disappeared and I got busy. Figured you'd gone for a ride and I'd tell you when you got back." He turned to pick up another bale.

"But why?"

"Economics."

"What economics?"

To Bob's way of thinking, answering questions asked was always the easiest way through a conversation. "The boss wasn't making enough to pay the bills so he sold out to a developer who's going to level the place and put up a bunch of condos, and he consigned the horses to the auction."

Paulie knew about bills. When she was helping stock shelves at her father's store she had heard him in his tiny office muttering about how he could juggle this money or that to pay this or that bill, especially in the past few years. She also knew about auctions. She'd gone with Bob to plenty of them because he'd told her learning about buying and selling stock was an important part of stable management.

Four days a week she mucked out the stalls and fed the horses. On weekends she also groomed horses and cleaned riding-school tack. In return, Bob paid her a small wage, taught her stable management and allowed her to exercise the horses whenever they weren't being used for lessons or rentals. It was a deal they'd struck after she'd spent a year hanging around the stable watching everything he did and asking endless questions.

Bob bought many of the stable's horses at auction. He'd shown her how to bid and what kind of tricks the sellers used to get the best prices for their stock. He'd shown her how to assess the animals for sale, too. She knew very well what kinds of horses were not bought by anyone who was looking for a horse to ride. Old horses, homely horses, horses with an 'attitude' — Duke kinds of horses.

"What'll happen to Duke?" she asked.

"Someone will buy him."

"Who?"

"Someone," he said, casually throwing another bale. The hay in the truck was three rows high now.

She didn't want to ask the question again, but she had to know. "Shoot it straight, Bob. Someone who?"

"Well, now," he said, "when you ask like that I guess it's only right to tell you. Chances are old Duke'll end up at Railway Three."

Paulie had known that would be the answer, but she was horrified to hear it all the same. "No! Duke's a good horse. He doesn't deserve that. They can't buy him! You have to do something!"

Bob hefted a huge bale and threw it down. It landed squarely in the top right corner of the truck, fourth row up. "I know you and him get along real good, Brat, but he ain't like that with everybody. He can be a cantankerous old buzzard. His Roman nose tells you that and he's twenty-five if he's a day. Chances are he won't last a whole lot longer anyway. Best for him to go before he gets all crippled up or someone mistreats him 'cause he's the way he is. The meat buyers are humane. He won't feel a thing."

"How can you say that?" Paulie shouted. "He might be twenty-five but he runs and bucks and plays like a two-year-old." Her eyes went to Bob's game leg and to his gnarled hands. "You're old and you're crippled and no one wants to put you in a dog food can!"

Bob took his time about answering. "Nope," he said at last, "no one does. But then I'm the one who pays to keep me."

Paulie sucked in her breath. "I'm sorry I said that. No I'm not. Duke doesn't know how old he's supposed to be. He's not too old." She tried to think and finally said, "Bob?"

"That's me."

"Could you buy Duke and then when I get the money I'll buy him from you? And in the meantime I'll take care of him."

He stopped tossing hay. "Well, that might be a plan. But I won't be here."

She was stunned. "Where will you be?"

"I'll be going north."

"North? What for? Why don't you stay here?" she blurted.

"Well, now I 'spect I would, but this city has moved all the way out into the country and it's gettin' so's a fella can't hardly breathe the air anymore, let alone afford the price of land here. North's where there's still plenty of open country and maybe some affordable land." His next words came slowly. "You take care and stay outta trouble, Brat."

"You, too," she said automatically.

"I will," he agreed, then added with a smile, "that is, unless it finds me."

Paulie laughed. It was a reminder of the first thing she'd ever said to him. She had been crouched on the top of a stall wall, leaning to grasp the wither of a horse she thought she'd just sit on for a moment. Just then Bob had opened the door of that particular stall and she'd toppled off the wall and into the feeder. Partially buried in hay, she had looked up from under the horse's startled nose into Bob's angry eyes and said, "Howdy, stranger. You must be the new stable manager. Sorry to be in your horse's food, but you know, sometimes trouble just finds me. My name's Paulie." Bob had howled with laughter and that had been the beginning of their three-year friendship. She didn't want him to go. But she knew that once Bob made up his mind to do something, he did it. "When are you leaving?" she asked in a morose tone.

"When everything's finished up here. Couple of days, I expect."

She blinked and barked out a declaration. "Well, even if you are going, I'm not going to let Railway Three get Duke."

"You're not, huh."

"No."

"Okay," he said, heaving another bale. It missed the truck and he swore.

There was nothing else to say. Paulie headed for the trapdoor and went down the ladder more slowly than she'd come up. She was thinking now. In spite of her bravado, she didn't know what she could do to save her favourite horse. Her father had told her every time she asked that he was not going to buy a horse. "Not now, and not anytime in the future," he'd said the last time she'd nagged him about it, "so you might as well give up on the idea." He'd told her her "horse thing" was becoming an obsession and that if she couldn't stop pestering him about it she'd have to stop going to the stables altogether. But surely if he knew the situation, that the auction was — oh no, it was tomorrow! She had practically no time at all.

She ran back to the pasture, but both Duke and the awful man were gone. She ran for her bike. Her parents would help her save Duke, she thought. They had to. She pedalled homeward as fast as she could.

— Two —

It was the approaching dark that made Paulie remember the time. The family would probably be sitting down to supper right now and she was late. Again. Her father's warning after the last time rang in her ear. "No more excuses," he'd said. "Next time you are not home when you are supposed to be home you will be grounded." As far as he was concerned, the evening meal was sacrosanct. It was the one time they could all sit down together and share things as a family, he said, and no child would be excused from being there. She pumped her burning legs harder.

Dropping her bike by the back door of her house, she ran in, peeling off her jacket as she came into the kitchen. Through the archway to the dining room she could see everyone except her mother was at the table eating. Her mother worked till seven on Saturdays.

As she walked into the dining room, her sister's voice squawked, "You're late!"

"Shut up," Paulie said. She surveyed the table. The bowls that had been filled with rice and vegetables were empty. On a platter there were a few pieces of chicken.

Her father laid his knife and fork on his plate, then wiped his mouth with his napkin. "I'm sorry, Paulie, but you are late, and you are grounded for the next three days," he said.

"No," Paulie said. "You can't … I mean, I'm sorry I'm late, but you …"

He held up his hand. "Stop."

"But it's not fair!" she cried. "You said I had to be home in time for supper. Well, I'm here and you're all still at the table. That's in time for supper."

"If you insist on arguing, we'll make it four days."

They'd been over this ground before. She knew he meant it. Fuming at his "obsession" and at herself, she forced herself to swallow her next words. She pulled out a chair.

"You can't sit on Mother's needlepoint stinking like that," her sister said. "You smell like manure. Can't you even wash before you come in here?"

Glaring at Gloria, Paulie unzipped her jeans.

"Paulie," her father said wearily, "we don't undress at the table and we don't come to the table undressed."

"All right, I'll go upstairs, as long as it doesn't mean I'll be too late to get anything to eat."

Her father sighed. "For heaven's sake, just go and change."

Paulie took the stairs three at a time, but by the time she got back everyone else had left the table. She grabbed a drumstick and went to the living room.

"Dad," she said to the book in front of her father's face, "I need to talk to you."

He lowered the book and waited.

Paulie hesitated. She didn't know how to begin. She took a long breath. "There's a problem ... sort of ... well, it's not really a problem if I ..." She started over. "Well, see, there's a horse that's going to be taken to the auction tomorrow and ... no, wait, Dad! This is important. This horse is going to be ... he's old, and Bob says probably nobody will buy him except the meat buyer. They'll kill him, and he's a wonderful horse. He is! If we could buy him I'd do anything. I'd do all the yard work, and anything else you said. I could get another job somewhere and help pay for him. I would even work at the store a lot more. Please, Dad."

Her father's face was set and sad. "Paulie, I don't know how many ways to say this to you. There are a lot of people in this family and every one of them needs things. Paying for a horse doesn't stop with buying one. Keeping one, especially in the city, is very, very expensive. We simply cannot afford it. I'm sorry about this horse of yours, but you never know what will happen at an auction. If he's as wonderful as you say he is, someone else will buy him."

"They won't," she said bitterly. "And I won't even be there because I'm grounded. Will you at least let me go to the auction tomorrow so I can maybe talk someone else into buying him?"

He considered. "All right. You can begin the grounding on Monday. Now go and do your homework, will you, and let me read."

"Homework?" Paulie protested. "It's only Saturday."

He glowered at her and she chewed her lip and left without saying any more.

Paulie's appetite was gone. She absently shoved the chicken into her shirt pocket and went upstairs. In her room she settled onto a large pillow on the floor, crossing her legs yoga style. A small orange and white cat came out from under her bed and purred toward her. The cat stuck her nose into Paulie's shirt, then tried to get the chicken. Paulie took it out, tore off some strips, and put them on one of her legs. While the cat purred and ate, Paulie stroked her fur. "You're lucky, Perfect," she told the cat. "You don't have to obey stupid rules and wait until you grow up before you'll get to do what you want to do." The cat's nose bumped against Paulie's palm and her rough tongue licked Paulie's fingers. "All you want is to eat regularly and be scratched," Paulie said, running her hand over the cat's smooth head. "Oh, Perfect, what am I gonna do? Duke will be bought by the meat buyers. I know it. Everyone thinks he's old and ugly. He's not ugly. He's … unique."

Gloria yelled up the stairs. "Get down here for dishes right now, Paulie! It's your night to wash."

"There's someone I'd like to put in a dog food can," Paulie told the cat, "but eating her would probably kill the poor dogs."

"You've got one minute!" Gloria hollered. "I mean it. One minute before I leave. This is your last warning."

Slowly Paulie uncoiled herself. She left Perfect curled contentedly in the centre of the big pillow and ambled down the stairs and into the kitchen.

"Too late," Gloria announced when Paulie appeared. "I'm gone."

Paulie had no energy for a fight with Gloria. "Go then," she said. She didn't have to say it more than once. Slowly she stacked the dishes and ran water into the sink. Twenty minutes later, when her mother walked into the kitchen, she was still there, playing with the soap bubbles.

"Penny for your thoughts, Paulie."

Paulie jumped.

"Sorry, I didn't mean to scare you. Daydreaming?"

"Huh? No. Well, sort of, I guess. Mom?"

"What?"

"Uh …there's a plate of dinner for you in the oven, I think."

"Yes, I see. Thank you. What kind of a day did you have?" her mother asked, carrying her plate to the kitchen table and sitting down.

"Dad grounded me and this time it definitely isn't fair."

"Isn't it?"

"No. If someone told you you had to be home by suppertime and you got here before anyone had left the table, wouldn't you think that meant you were here by suppertime?"

"I think," her mother said between mouthfuls of rice, "this is something between you and your father."

Paulie changed the subject. "Mom, how much money do you make at your job?"

Her mother smiled. "What's this all about?"

"Something important. This is important, Mom."

"I can see that," her mother said gently. "What's so important?"

"I need some money to buy a horse. Don't look like that. Just listen to me, please. Duke's going to be sold at the auction and Bob says he's going to be bought by the meat buyer because no one else will buy him."

"Why doesn't Bob think anyone else will buy him?"

"Because Duke's old and, well, he has a few what you might call ... quirks. For instance, sometimes he likes to step on some people's feet."

Her mother laughed. "I can see where that might make him unpopular. But you never know what will happen at an auction, Paulie. All kinds of people go to auctions."

Paulie shook her head. "Bob's sure Duke will go to Railway Three and Bob knows. So if I don't buy him Duke doesn't have a chance."

"Honey, I'm sorry about the horse, but I'm afraid I just can't help you right now. The money I make at the craft store goes to Willie for his school expenses."

"Willie! Everything goes to Willie!" Paulie cried. As soon as she said it she was ashamed. She knew how hard her parents worked for all of them. Red spots flamed in her cheeks.

"Your turn will come, Paulie," her mother said softly.

Paulie let the shame kindle to full-blown anger and aimed it at her mother. "I don't want my turn to come!" she shouted, yanking her hands out of the sink. "It'll be too late when my stupid turn comes! Duke'll be dead, can't you understand that?" She didn't wait for a reply. She tore from the room and up the stairs to her bedroom. She slammed the door shut. The cat woke up and scuttled under Paulie's bed. Paulie was too angry to notice she'd frightened the cat, or to be sorry. She ignored Perfect, who eventually came out and padded back onto her lap. Paulie stroked her. With each stroke she grew calmer. The furrow in her brow relaxed but she didn't stop thinking. At length she got up and went to her parents' bedroom. The door was open and the room was empty. She went in, closed the door, and picked up the telephone.

"Hi, Grandma," she said after her grandmother had said hello.

"Hello, Pauline."

Some silence elapsed; then Paulie said, "Grandma, can I ask you a question?"

"Of course. What is it?"

"Could you loan me some money?"

She was beginning to think the line had gone dead when her grandmother spoke again. "How much money did you have in mind?"

"Well, I need it to buy a horse and ... "

"Oh dear, horses again. So your parents have changed their minds about your having one, have they?"

"Not exactly, but this is …"

Again her grandmother interrupted her. "Pauline, you know very well I will not provide you with something that is against your parents' wishes."

"You don't understand," Paulie started. "I just want …"

"I do understand." Her grandmother's voice was sharp. "Now, let's just drop the subject, shall we? We'll pretend this conversation didn't happen."

Paulie sighed. "Is Nana there?" Nana was Grandma's mother.

"She is, but she's resting so I won't wake her right now."

Paulie was alarmed. "Is she sick?"

"Oh, no, she's just getting on and she needs more rest than she used to, that's all. Is there a message you'd like me to give her?"

"No."

"Well, then, we'll see you tomorrow when we come for supper, won't we."

"Yes, Grandma, see you soon." Paulie hung up and returned to her room. She had gone over and over her bank book. In the past two years she had put most of her wages from the stable into her account. She had $276.75 saved up. It wasn't enough to buy feed, let alone a horse. Even if it was enough, she couldn't get at it until Monday. Her parents had said she was too young to have a plastic card that would let her take money from an electronic teller, and her bank would be closed tomorrow. All the banks would. And auctioneers did not take promises or IOUs. They took only cash, certified cheques or money orders.

She had to have money. Duke didn't deserve to die, no matter how many times her parents had told her they couldn't afford a horse. Anyway, she wasn't asking them to buy him, but would they listen? Would anyone listen to her, ever? No. Well, no one but Nana. Nana might be old and need her rest, but she knew how to treat a kid. She always listened. And she was smart. *She's my last hope*, Paulie thought. *But she lives with Grandma. Maybe she doesn't have any money of her own.* Aware that she would have to get by her grandmother, Paulie told herself, *I have to ask.*

— Three —

ana was an early riser and the auction started at one. Before six a.m. Paulie was up and making good time to her grandmother's house three blocks away. When she got there, she went around to the backyard where a solarium and Nana's room had been added to the old house. The addition had been Grandma's idea when Nana moved back in with her, and now, Nana said, she had grown used to the privacy it provided them both. Her entrance was her own and she even had a small, private patio where she entertained her friends when the weather warranted.

Paulie would give anything to have quarters like Nana's, separate from the main house. Even having her own room *in* her house would be an improvement over sharing a room with Gloria. For one thing, Paulie liked to have her stuff spread around where she could see it. It made her feel like she was actually living in a place instead of just passing through. Gloria's things were always "arranged." In the closet, she hung her skirts, tops, dresses and pants in groupings based on colour. Her sweaters were folded on closet shelves and her T-shirts and sweatshirts were folded on the shelves she designated expressly for "casual" wear, again grouped for colour. Even the underwear in her drawers was folded! One or two little pieces of Paulie's clothing on the floor, and Gloria went berserk. Grandma, Paulie knew, was a neatnik, too, and Nana, like Paulie, was not.

Nana was watering plants in the solarium. Paulie spotted her at the same time Nana saw Paulie. The door in the solarium opened. "Pink!" Nana greeted her. "What a nice time for you to come. I was just going to have breakfast. I've got some banana and chocolate chip muffins I baked yesterday. Would you like to join me for a picnic on the patio?"

Paulie remembered she had forgotten to eat breakfast and Nana's banana and chocolate chip muffins were the best in the world. "I could eat a dozen!" she said.

Nana laughed. She set her watering can on a sill and bustled through the door to her room as quickly as her old legs would take her. Paulie followed. Although it was still full of familiar things, Nana's room looked somehow different. Something was missing. "Nana," Paulie said while her eyes looked around, "where are all your gems?"

For as long as Paulie could remember, Nana's lifetime collection of stones and shells had covered the top of every chest and table in the room. When she was a small child, Paulie had spent hours sorting and fingering the collection. The shimmering pinky whiteness of the inside of the oyster shells had felt silkier to her than her grandmother's satin sheets. She could hear the ocean in the conch shells. At least, that was what Nana had told her the sound was. Paulie had never seen the ocean, but Nana's stories and that sound made her dream about it. Smooth black agates, cool green jade, and rough ice-coloured crystals had drawn her eyes and hands, too. Paulie had called them gems and the name had stuck. But now the bureaus and tables were bare, dusted clean. Something else was missing, too. It took Paulie a minute to realize what. "And your baskets? What happened to your baskets?"

Nana's face twisted into a troubled frown. "Oh, dear. I suppose I put them someplace and have forgotten where. I seem to be forgetting more and more things."

"You forgot where you put your baskets of reeds and grasses?"

"No, Dorothy took those away because the grasses kept shedding on the carpet. They were very dry and Dorothy's afraid of fire. I'm afraid I've forgotten just where I put my gems."

Paulie was dismayed at the look in her great-grand-mother's eyes. It was as if she had a pain somewhere, but couldn't locate its source. "Don't worry, Nana," she said, "I'll help you look for your gems. We'll find them."

"That would be lovely, dear. But first we'll have our picnic, shall we?"

It suited Paulie. Her stomach was rumbling. She waited while Nana located the cookie tin she wanted and took it down from the shelf. "Now a nice pot of tea…"

"I'll make that," Paulie offered. "Rosehip?"

"That would be just right," Nana answered.

Paulie filled Nana's copper kettle in the small bathroom that adjoined the larger room. She brought the full kettle back into the big room and put it on a hot plate that sat on a marble-top table which stood under the shelves where Nana kept her company dishes, cookie tins, teas and a few other food things. Nana had set her blue-heron teapot and two tea bags on the table beside the hotplate.

When the brew was ready, Paulie carried it and two blue-heron mugs outside and set them on the patio table, where Nana had already put a plateful of muffins.

"Isn't it a wonderful morning," her great-grandmother said as she bit into a clump of chocolate chips.

Paulie was too busy chewing to answer so she just nodded her own contentment. She loved it out here and she loved the way Nana ate food, like every bite was the most delicious thing she had ever tasted. Of course, the muffins were! She was reluctant to break the mood, but when she'd finished her second muffin she sat forward, took a deep breath, and plunged ahead.

"Nana, I really came over to ask you something," she said. "It's a really big favour and I want you to say no if you want to," she added.

Nana smiled. "What is this very big favour, Pink?"

"I was wondering, do you have any money?"

"Why, yes. Would you like it?"

Paulie jerked with surprise. "Well," she said, "I'd like to borrow it until tomorrow because tomorrow the bank is open and I can get my own money. Would that be all right?"

"Of course, dear. You keep it for as long as you like."

"Don't you want to know why I want it?" Paulie asked.

"You can tell me if you like, but I'll just go and get it first, shall I." She got shakily to her feet.

Paulie sat and waited while her great-grandmother went back to her bedroom. It seemed like forever before she came back carrying a tin cigar box.

"Here we are," Nana said, opening the box. No one in the family had smoked cigars since Great-Grandpa had died, long before Paulie was born, and Nana often told Paulie she missed the smell of a good cigar, but she didn't miss the smoke. As old as the box was, Paulie could smell cigars when Nana opened it. Nana stretched out her hand holding what looked to Paulie to be about fifty dollars. "You keep this for as long as you need it," Nana said.

Paulie stared at the bills. "Oh, Nana," she got out at last, "I'm sorry. I ... uh ... it's ... it's not enough. I should have told you."

"Well," Nana said kindly, "suppose you tell me now?"

"I need it to buy a horse," Paulie explained. "I have two hundred and seventy-six dollars, but I can't get it until Monday and the horse I want to buy is going to be auctioned this afternoon." She stopped and chewed her lip. "I...I asked Mom but she has to send her money to Willie for university, and Dad, uh, he doesn't really want me to buy a horse at all. But if I don't buy him, Nana, he'll go to the meat buyer probably, and then he'll be killed. I don't know if what I have will even be enough to buy him, but I have to try!" She groaned. "I wish I had a bank card so I could get my own money."

Nana was flustered. "Oh dear. I'm so sorry, Pink. Dorothy doesn't think it's a good idea for me to keep very much money in the house and I'm afraid this is all I have here."

Paulie saw the hurt in her great-grandmother's face, and suddenly the lines seemed so much more numerous and deeper than they had; her eyes more sunken, and her skin so pale. Nana was old. She must be very tired. Her grandmother had been right; Paulie shouldn't have pestered Nana with her problems. "Don't be sorry, Nana," she said. "Don't worry. It's all right. I'll …"

"Mother," Paulie's grandmother's voice sounded in the solarium, "who are you talking to? Oh, my, Pauline. I didn't expect anyone to be visiting this early. It is a little early, don't you think?"

"Nonsense," Nana smiled. "It's especially nice to see Pink first thing in the morning. We were just having a picnic. Would you like to take some hot tea and a muffin with us, Dorothy?"

"No, thank you," Paulie's grandmother replied. "If you're coming to church this morning, I think we'd better wash your hair now so it will dry and I'll have time to curl it."

"I don't believe I will go today, dear."

Concern showed on Paulie's grandmother's face. "Are you feeling unwell, Mother?"

"No, dear. I'm fine. I have some things I'd like to do. I do want to look for my gems. Paulie was asking about them.

What do you think I might have done with them?"

"I told you I put them in a box in the closet of the room next to mine."

"Oh … yes … I suppose you did tell me. Would you bring them down, Dorothy?"

"Mother, we've talked about that several times and we decided it would be best to leave them there, where they won't get broken or dusty, for now. When you move into that room, we'll unpack them again and set them up as you like them."

There was a long, awkward silence. Paulie broke it. "I think maybe I'd better go home now." She hugged her great-grandmother and her grandmother. "Bye, Nana. Bye, Grandma."

On the way home, Paulie stepped across a crack in the sidewalk and absently repeated a rhyme: "Step on a crack, break your mother's back." The rhyme didn't make sense. Nothing made sense anymore. Nana was the oldest, yet Grandma bossed her around. Everyone bossed Paulie around. What was she going to do now about Duke? She wished her uncles and aunt lived here. If they did she'd have more people to ask and maybe, just maybe, one of them would help. But wishing was stupid because they didn't live here and even if she phoned them they wouldn't be able to get money to her in time to help her with Duke. Her hope had all but gone.

— *Four* —

By noon Paulie was beside herself. Her brother Sam said he only had $1.13 in his money jar and Jerry was only four. He had no money at all. Gloria said if she had any money to loan, which she didn't, she would charge fifty percent interest seeing as it was Paulie who wanted it. Willie was no bet since Mom had said she had to send her money to him. Paulie would have asked her friends, especially Jenny, but they had told her often enough their allowances lasted only as long as it took them to get to the movies or the mall. Usually they borrowed from Paulie, who was the only one of them who worked for actual money.

She got up to go upstairs. Sometimes she kept a few dollars in a coffee can she kept on her closet shelf. Maybe she'd forgotten a stash she'd put there. She hadn't, and when she clumped back down the stairs her mother, who was in the living room working on a quilt, spoke to her.

"Paulie, you've been up and down those stairs half a dozen times in the last half hour. Can't you find something to do with yourself?"

Paulie came and sat on the chesterfield across from her mother's chair. She watched her fingers push the needle and thread in and out. The needle danced. Her mother was making a quilt of the galaxy. Midnight blue, covered with silver stars. Finished pieces were stacked on the floor beside her chair. To Paulie, it seemed there were hundreds of pieces, all different shapes. It always amazed her how her mother knew exactly where to put each piece to make beautiful patterns. Paulie had made one quilt. It had been small with a simple design, but still the pieces of the design hadn't matched properly and the quilt ended up looking cockeyed. But Perfect, whom she'd given it to for Christmas, liked it.

She sighed. And sighed again, which made her mother sigh. "There's a large ball of mixed silk threads in my basket, Paulie. How would you like to separate them into weights and colours for me?"

"I wouldn't!" Paulie snapped.

Her mother looked up. "I don't think there's any call for that tone of voice."

"Well, I think there is," Paulie said, "but no one around here cares what I think." Before her mother could reply she was out the front door and running. She passed the last two houses on her block, and plowed through the tall grass and the weeds that choked the vacant lot. She passed the crumbling open basement of the church that had been torn down. Two blocks farther on, she turned east. She sped past houses and trees, past the new church, past the Victoria Street Daycare/Community Centre. In the next block, she ran past her father's neighbourhood store. Her sneakers slapped the pavement. She was heading out of town. Her breath came in shorter and shorter pants. Finally, out of breath, she walked.

Eventually she found herself at the auction. She hadn't intended to come here. If she couldn't buy Duke, she sure didn't want to sit in the stands and watch some ghoulish meat buyer get him. But her feet dragged her into the building.

Across from where she stood, there was a doorway leading to a large arena. Inside the arena was a sales ring. The sales ring was really a rectangle, surrounded on three sides by bleachers. At the end of the ring farthest from the entrance to the arena were a raised auctioneer's booth and two ramps leading to two doors. Animals that were to be auctioned came in one door and after they were sold they were sent up the other ramp — out into holding pens to wait to be loaded into crates or onto trucks. Right now there were no animals either coming into or going out of the sales ring. In the centre of the ring, an auctioneer's helper stood beside several boxes of assorted junk. Bob said the auctioneers sold the junk to give people time to loosen up their fingers so they could pull out real money when it came time to buy the animals.

The people who were in the stands now apparently weren't spending too much. The auctioneer was working hard to get them to bid. "It's only money," he was saying. "You can always go out and make some more, so come on, get off your hands. Lookee here at this good dehorner. Nigel, hold up that dehorner so the folks up top can get a good look. Wouldn't get better'n that at your best friend's hardware store. Twenny gimmeetwenny gimmeetwenny gimmeetwenny, nineteen then. Nineteen starts 'er. ... Fifteen then. Fourteen. I'm not gonna give it away, folks, so you might as well bid." No one, it seemed, was interested in the excellent dehorner. "Okay," the auctioneer said, "put it away, Nigel. We'll sell it next Wednesday to the rich folks." The crowd tittered.

Paulie walked down the aisleway that ran behind the bleachers on the left side of the ring. At the end of the passage was yet another door. She stepped out into the sunshine, to the stockyards and a maze of holding pens. In the pen closest to the building, pigs that had only that morning been weaned from their mothers were milling and squealing while two men with hooked gaffs separated them according to size. A third man, stationed near the "IN RAMP," prodded the smallest pigs through the door and into the arena. These "weaner-pigs" would be the first animals sold today.

Next was a pen full of goats. Inside this enclosure a woman was checking the goats' feet and udders and writing things on a sheet of paper clipped to a board. In a corner of the pen two does rose up on their hind legs and butted heads. The woman, one of the auction staff, Paulie knew, laughed and looked up. She said hello to Paulie. Paulie nodded and kept moving.

Small black and white calves occupied the next two pens. Males taken off their mothers so the dairy farmers would have their mothers' milk. Most of them were on their feet, bawling. A few lay on their sides in the scanty sawdust, their legs tucked close to their bodies. Occasionally these, too, lifted their muzzles and bawled. Paulie knew they would end up as veal.

Someone was packing Rhode Island Red chickens into wooden crates. Unable to move sideways, or up, or down, the chickens poked their heads out between the slats and pecked at one another with their sharp curved beaks. Beside these crates a young couple stood discussing how old the Banties and the exotic Silkies, packed ten to a crate, might be. Paulie didn't listen. Next to the chicken crates the horse paddocks began.

There were four cedar-railed horse paddocks. Most of the horses were jammed into two of them while the remaining two held a single horse each. Paulie didn't know why the bay had been separated from the other horses, but the chestnut mare in the farthest paddock stood with her legs splayed apart and her head low to the ground. She was razor-back thin. Bob had told Paulie any horse who looked and stood like that was very sick. Paulie knew a vet had to certify any animal to be auctioned as healthy before it could be sold here. She wondered if the vet had seen that mare.

Duke was in the second paddock, standing with his chin resting on the withers of one of his old stablemates. His eyes were almost closed. He flicked an ear and moved closer to the body of his friend. He looked relaxed, Paulie thought, like he was spending the morning on the beach enjoying one of the last days of a beautiful Indian summer. She wanted to go to him, to wrap her arms around his neck, to blow her breath into his nose, to lead him to an open field of short brown grass where he could roll: head back, hooves waving, while he scratched his sensitive skin with nature's brush. But she couldn't. She could not say goodbye, either.

She wound her way back toward the building, acutely aware that the red number stuck to Duke's right hip was 111. When he left the sales ring, a black number on a white background would be on his other hip. It would be the buyer's number.

If only there were some way ... but there wasn't. She knew that. She should leave, go somewhere where her chest and stomach wouldn't hurt so much. She stopped, blocked by the men with gaffs. They were opening metal gates, closing others; forming new pens and new runways as gates locked into place. The weaner pigs, marked now with buyers' numbers, were squealing up the exit ramp of the sales ring and into another holding pen. They milled in a tight circle, a swarming mass of frantic flesh not knowing where to go. The gate to their pen opened and they were driven down a runway that led to a smaller pen where they would be separated according to their numbers and then put in crates or on trucks to be carted home by their new owners. Like an army of ants heading to a picnic, the pigs advanced, oinking and snorting, mercifully unaware yet that they would someday be the main dish at a human's table.

When the changes were complete, Paulie was allowed to pass. She made for the door that led back to the welcome dimness under the bleachers, fighting to hold back her tears. She kept her head down, seeing nothing until someone spoke to her.

"Goodness, Pink, you are in a hurry."

Paulie started and looked up to see her great-grandmother's smiling eyes. "Nana! What are you doing here? I mean, it's great you're here, but how…? Is Grandma here?"

"Oh, my goodness, no."

"Then how did you come?"

"I took a taxi."

"Oh. But how did you know I was here?" Paulie couldn't believe it. She hadn't even known she was coming herself.

Again Nana's eyes cracked into a smile. "I telephoned to speak to you and your mother told me you'd gone out. I had a hunch this was where you'd be."

"How did you know where to look for me?"

"I looked several places and then asked a very nice gentleman where else I might look. He told me where you were. He seemed to know you."

"Well, some of the staff know me because I've been here pretty often with Bob," Paulie said.

"Do you mind if we go and sit somewhere?" Nana said.

"We can sit there." Paulie pointed to an empty spot on one of the bleachers.

"Ah, that looks fine."

As she settled herself onto the seat, Nana inhaled sharply.

"You know," she said, "I'd almost forgotten just how pungent a barn can be."

Paulie thought of Gloria's constant complaints about what she called Paulie's "stinking contamination" of their room, but to Paulie horse sweat, green hay and oat straw overlaid with oiled leather odours called up the outdoors and a physicality she loved. Even the manure smell didn't bother her. "Don't you like it, Nana?" she asked.

Nana smiled. "When I was your age, I often tried to convince my father and mother to let me sleep in the barn, but they didn't think it was a very good idea. Sometimes I did, though."

"You had a barn? I thought you always lived in the city."

Nana laughed. "When I was young, the city was still very like the country. Almost everyone kept chickens and a cow or two and perhaps some pigs. It wasn't until your grandmother's girlhood that people stopped doing that, and even then those who lived on the outskirts of the city kept some animals. Now though," she added wistfully, "it's not legal to keep farm animals anywhere near the city."

"I'd like to live on a farm," Paulie said.

They were called to attention when the auctioneer announced the beginning of the sale of calves. "Bob says you can tell what the price of the steers and horses will be by the price of the calves," Paulie said. "He says what people bid for the calves tells you what kind of mood the crowd is in. Have you been to an auction before, Nana?"

"Oh, goodness, yes. My father took me with him every Saturday when he went to the auction. Our neighbours said he was the one who could always get stock for the best price and so they would give him their funds and he bought what animals they wanted for them."

The auctioneer's voice over the loudspeakers cut them off. "This here's prime stock," he said. "Pedigreed from your fingertips to your armpits. These little bulls will gain so much weight so fast that by the time you butcher 'em you'll need a two-ton lift just to get 'em on the table."

"You mean we'll need it to lift the bull you're flinging," someone yelled. "Them skinny things is rejects."

The crowd laughed.

"Forty-five starts 'em," the auctioneer said. "Forty-five forty-five endive nojive forty-five gimmeeforty-five," he sang. "All right, forty. Forty cents. Thirty-five then, let's get this thing going."

"Thirty-one," a voice rang and the bidding had begun.

The price climbed slowly back to forty-three before the auctioneer's gavel banged. "Sold at forty-three cents a pound." He nodded to a man in the third row on the left side. "How many you want at that price, Cliff?"

"All of them," the man said.

It was too high, Paulie thought. Duke weighed about twelve-hundred pounds. At forty-three cents a pound, a meat buyer would be willing to pay 516 dollars for him. Even if she had her money from the bank, it wouldn't be enough. Inside, she slumped.

"Isn't this exciting," Nana said. "It takes me right back to when I was a little girl."

"Sold all to number six, Cliff Mape," the auctioneer said.

Forgetting to turn off his microphone, he leaned toward the clerk sitting to his right. "Put it on his tab," he told the clerk.

Paulie had heard that expression before. It meant that the man who had bought the calves could pay for them later. If he could do that, Paulie thought, so could she. Catching some of her great-grandmother's excitement, she forgot about how high the price had gone. "Nana, I've got to go to the office. I think maybe I can get them to let me wait awhile to pay, and if they will, maybe I can still buy Duke."

"There's always an extra price to pay for credit, Pink," Nana said.

Paulie's brown eyes shone. "But it would be worth it. I'd pay anything."

"I'll come with you," Nana said.

At the office Nana stood near the door. Paulie went to the registration desk. "I'd like a number," she said to the girl behind the desk.

The girl was busy adding columns of figures. With her eyes on the computer keyboard, she pulled a piece of paper off a stack and pushed it, along with a pen, across to Paulie. "Fill out this form. Make sure you read the fine print. When you've finished, bring it back."

Paulie moved to a counter along the opposite wall. She filled in all the blanks, including her birth date. She read the rules. Number two said: *Only persons who have reached the legal age of majority are eligible to bid.* She didn't know what that meant, but she had a feeling she didn't want to ask. She signed her name and returned to the desk.

A door behind the girl's desk opened and Paulie could see the back of the auctioneer and the back of the podium. The clerk put his head through the door. "Hurry up with that stack, will you, Linda?"

"I'm hurrying," Linda fired back.

Paulie put her paper on the desk and the girl pushed a number across to her. "There's a charge if it isn't returned," she said, her fingers rapidly clicking keys on the number pad of her computer keyboard. "Rats!" she muttered, shaking her head.

"I need to arrange a tab," Paulie said.

"Do you have a line of credit with us?"

"No," Paulie said.

"Linda!" the man pushed.

"Yeah, yeah, I'm coming already!" Her fingers flew faster. "There's a six percent charge for credit," she said to Paulie. "The item must be picked up before eleven a.m. tomorrow. If it isn't, it will be auctioned at the next sales date and if it sells for less than you paid, you'll be charged the difference plus the six percent. Sign here," she droned, marking an "x" on the back side of Paulie's paper. She finally raised her head and squinted upward at an earnest young face framed by a shining mop of gold-brown hair. "You don't look eighteen?"

"Linda!" the clerk sounded annoyed.

"Hey, I'm working here as fast as I can. You wanna come down here and do it faster?" The door closed. The girl returned her attention to Paulie. "I can't let you have a number unless you're eighteen."

"I'll sign for the number," Nana said.

"Okay, fine. You understand that by signing you are responsible for the debt if she doesn't pay, Ma'am?"

Nana nodded "yes" and was told to put her address and phone number on the form, and it was done.

"Would you like to get something to eat, Pink?" Nana asked.

The thought of food gagged Paulie. "No."

"Well then," Nana said, "we'll wait."

The suggestion of food brought another thought to Paulie's mind. Supper and her father's edict. "Nana," she said with a new urgency, "We're supposed to be home for supper and the horses are never auctioned until after the supper break."

Nana patted Paulie's arm. "That will be all right. I'll telephone and let them know you and I are enjoying an evening out. You go and get us our seats back."

"Thanks, Nana," Paulie said, sure she would never be able to thank her great-grandmother enough. Inside her jacket pocket, her fingers kept pinching the plastic number.

— *Five* —

It was six-thirty. The horses still had not come up for auction, but the stands were getting crowded. The auctioneers were having their supper break. Paulie kept watching the people come in and wished they'd stop. The more people there were, the higher the prices would go. "Auctioneers love full houses," Bob had said. "A full house means more money on hand; more bidding, higher prices." As she and others shuffled sideways to make room for two more people to squeeze onto her bench, the money in her bank account was seeming like less and less. Nana stirred and got stiffly to her feet. "I'm going to go for a little walk, dear. Would you like a bite to eat now?"

"Maybe," Paulie said, though she really didn't think she would be able to eat anything. Her stomach felt as if it were full of coiling snakes. She pictured the canteen. "It will be awfully crowded in the concession right now, Nana.

Are you sure you want to go? I'll go and you can stay here if you like?"

"No, no, it will be very good for me to walk. These old legs can get rather stiff if I sit too long."

Unconsciously, Paulie dropped her eyes. Below the hem of her coat, Nana's legs were wrapped in thick elastic stockings, but even through the stockings, Paulie could see the bumps and bulges of the varicose veins Nana never mentioned. Paulie's father had varicose veins. She knew they hurt. Nana's legs must be really hurting, Paulie thought. They should leave. But she couldn't suggest it. She had to stay. "Are you having an okay time, Nana?" she asked.

"I'm having a wonderful time. Are you, Pink?"

Paulie looked around. "There are too many people now," she confessed.

Nana nodded. "There do seem to be quite a few. How about a cup of hot soup?" she prodded.

"All right," Paulie said doubtfully. She took off her jacket and put it on Nana's spot. "Don't worry, I'll keep your seat," she assured her great-grandmother.

When Nana returned and they were drinking cups of chicken soup and eating egg salad sandwiches, Paulie wished the auctioneer would get on with selling the horses. And then, when the door at the top of the in-ramp opened and Duke appeared, she wished they wouldn't do it at all. She hadn't expected to see Duke first. The man at the top of the ramp slapped the horse's rump, sending him down at a trot. When Duke got to the bottom, two more staff members took turns waving their arms at him to keep him moving. The auctioneer started his spiel. "This grey is a smooth-mouthed gelding. Been a riding school pony for years. Had vet attention and is certified healthy. Works just like a rocking horse, I'll bet. Put your saddle on him and just set there lettin' him rock you back and forth. I'll bet he sings lullabies, too. Says here his name's Duke."

Duke stopped moving and stood in the centre of the ring, trembling. His head went down; his eyes drooped. He stopped trembling and drooped further, looking totally lacklustre. "Start 'im at two hundred. Who will give me two hundred to buy a Duke for their youngster? Two hundred ... Come on now, you folks pay more than that for a dud and this here horse is a royal Duke," the auctioneer chanted.

"Some Duke!" the same voice that had shouted before yelled. "He can't even stand up straight."

One of the staff walked up to the horse and casually picked up each of his feet. He walked behind Duke and grabbed hold of his tail, pulled it, and swacked his rump. Duke barely moved. "Lookee there," said the auctioneer. "You could put your girlfriend or your mother on that horse and he'd bring 'em home safe. What more could you ask of a horse?"

This was not the Duke Paulie knew. She remembered the chestnut mare she had seen in the holding pen and groaned. What if Duke had picked up whatever was wrong with her?

"All right, seeing as I've just had supper and am in a good mood, one hundred dollars will start us off," the auctioneer continued good-naturedly. "Let's go now. We've gotta be outta here by midnight, folks."

Paulie saw the flip of a finger from a man standing near a corner of the ring. She'd seen him at auctions before. "He's from Railway Three," she whispered to Nana. "They're the meat buyers."

"One hundred I've got. Onefifty onefifty onefifty ain'titnifty onefifty. Twennyfive then. Come on, don't be shy. Onetwenny then. Twenny gimmeetwenny gimmeetwenny addapenny gimmeetwenny…"

Paulie's hand, holding her number, shot up.

"One twenty," the auctioneer nodded at her. "Now fifty."

The man from Railway Three tipped his hat.

"Seventy-five?" the auctioneer said to Paulie.

Paulie nodded.

"Two hunnerd now. Mentionaloverwhoain'tgottwo hunnerd anI'llshowyoualoverain'tgotagirl," he rattled off in a singsong spiel. "Twohunnerd is the number folks. Ante up."

One of the men in the ring bent and picked up a handful of sawdust that he threw at Duke in an effort to get him moving. Duke reacted with a half jump sideways, then slumped again. Paulie knew an action like that normally would have made the horse buck across the ring. "You can take this fella anywhere," the auctioneer said, "do anything with him. He'll babysit your kids, for Pete's sake. Two hundred, that's a quarter what you'd pay for a nanny for a month. And he'll only cost it once."

A man in a red-and-black plaid jacket and sitting beside a little boy raised a number.

The auctioneer smiled. "Got it. Two-fifty now." The auctioneer looked at Paulie. "Nice horse like this. Talk to your momma and your papa there. Get 'em to fork over some more of their money." The crowd laughed and Paulie grinned in spite of herself.

"Two twenty-five," she said clearly.

"Oh ho!" the auctioneer cried. "This little lady's been around. She knows what she's doing." Paulie turned red. "Okay, now fifty?" he cocked his head at Railway Three. The meat buyer said, "Yup."

The master salesman turned his attention to Paulie. "Two fifty to you, little lady. It's your turn. Seventy-five now."

Paulie took a deep breath. Would the meat buyer stop? Even if he did, she would have nothing left for feed or anything else. She didn't even know where she was going to put the horse, or how she'd get him there. She looked up at the man who had bid only once sitting beside the little boy. If she could only get Duke, maybe she could work something out with them. She nodded slowly.

"Three hunnerd," the auctioneer said, looking at his friend the meat buyer. Paulie saw the buyer glance at the auctioneer and then at her. Her heart sank. It was an old game. She was young and green and they were playing with her. They thought she would continue to go higher to get the horse. Railway Three smiled sideways and did his finger flip.

"Young man," Nana was on her feet, her voice loud and clear.

The auctioneer lowered his hand-held microphone, his eyes wide. "Oh, dear," Nana said quietly as if suddenly realizing what she was doing. Out of the corner of her eye she saw Paulie's raised, surprised face. The stands were pin-drop quiet. She carried on, addressing her question to the meat buyer. "Excuse me, but do you think you will be purchasing many horses tonight?" The man from Railway Three looked as if he'd been stunned with a ray gun. Nana stiffened a little more and went on, "Because if you do, perhaps you should let Pink here have this one. He's really not very fat."

The crowd hooted and cheered. All eyes turned on the meat buyer, who was still staring at Nana. Finally he grinned. "Withdraw," he said.

The auctioneer recovered himself, rolled out a barrel-deep guffaw, then sang, "Two hundred seventy-five once, twice, gone. Sold to the little lady with the ponytail. Hold up your number, honey."

The crowd went wild. The colour of Paulie's neck deepened to burgundy and spread upward into her cheeks, but she raised her number high. She watched the ring crew chase Duke up the out-ramp and knew he'd be in the pens for sold animals now, wearing her number. She was dazed, unable to believe it had really happened. She turned and hugged Nana hard.

Another horse appeared on the in-ramp. The auction resumed, but it was only a dull din in Paulie's ears. Duke was hers. But now what?

— Six —

aulie went to turn in her number. When she came back to the arena, she explained to Nana that she needed to talk to the other man, the one who was not from Railway Three but who had also bid on Duke. She couldn't see the man, so she made her way across the stands to where the boy still sat. She asked the boy if the man in the red-and-black plaid jacket was his father. "No," the boy answered, "he's not my dad. My dad's loading the truck." Paulie wished she had made it a point to look at the man's number. She was beginning to feel panicky. True, she had until eleven o'clock tomorrow morning before Duke had to be moved, but that didn't help much.

A long-ago lesson from Bob came into her head. She and Duke had been poised on the upper edge of a steep gully and she was afraid and showing it. "No, no, no," Bob had said. "Feel how that horse is bunched up under your fear. If you panic wha'd'ya think he's gonna do? Pop, that's what. Pop like a Jack-in-the-box and maybe you'll both go end over end. You hold him where he is — steady pressure with your legs and your hands quiet — and think your way through it. Then let him make the move. One step at a time. Act like you know where you're goin' and you'll get there." Fine, she thought now, but what if you couldn't see where you were supposed to go and you weren't sure at all that you *were* going to get there?

She went back to Nana, who looked cold and tired. "Nana, I can't go home yet. Should I call you a taxi?"

"I am a little tired," Nana said, "but I don't want to leave you here by yourself, Pink."

"It's all right. I'll call Bob."

"Then I'll just stay here with you until he arrives." The look on Nana's face said there'd be no argument. Paulie and her father were not the only ones in the family with a stubborn streak.

Paulie resigned herself. "I'll go and call him, then." She went to the pay phone, plugged in a quarter, and dialled the small office/bunkhouse that Bob had called home for the last ten years. After five rings an answering machine clicked in. Paulie left a message. Then she didn't know what else to do, so she asked Nana if she'd like to go and meet Duke, and took her great-grandmother outside.

In spite of it being a black night, the area around the holding pens was lit with huge floodlights that turned night into day. Trucks and trailers backed up to ramps where people were loading animals of all sizes and shapes for their various journeys. Paulie kept looking around for the man who had bid against her. If she could find him, maybe she could convince him to take the horse for what she had paid, or even for what he had bid. She would pay the difference. As long as it meant Duke was going to a good home. That is, if Duke wasn't sick. She'd almost forgotten about his strange behaviour in the ring. If he was sick, then what? She chewed her lip. "One step at a time," she reminded herself. "Duke will be over here," she told Nana.

Inside the enclosure, a small man stood at Duke's side. A hat the colour of dried tree bark was on his head, the battered brim pulled forward and down until it almost obscured his face. His faded jean jacket and blue jeans and the soft, worn leather of his brown boots said his clothes had seen a lot of wear.

"Bob!" Paulie shouted louder than she meant to, as relief filled her. "That's Bob," she told Nana, urging her to a faster pace. "How did you get here so fast? I only left my message five minutes ago."

When Bob saw Nana, he tilted the hat back on his head out of respect, revealing a face that looked as worn and comfortable as his clothes. The lines around his blue eyes crinkled to life. A straw he was chewing moved with his words. "I've been around," he said. "Saw you buy old Duke."

"You did?"

"Yup."

"You saw the whole thing?" Paulie wanted to know. She felt her face and neck get hot again.

"Mostly."

"Did you see the number of the man in the red and black plaid jacket who bid that one time?"

"Yup."

She allowed herself to breathe, then hesitated. In order to say what she was going to say, she would have to admit to Bob she had bought Duke without knowing how she was going to take care of him. She stammered. "I ... thought maybe I could talk to him; maybe give Duke to him for what he wanted to pay. I'd only lose seventy-five dollars and then Duke would have a real home."

"You think that fella would give him a home?" Bob asked, curious.

This brought Paulie's thoughts to an abrupt halt. She didn't know anything about the man. She'd only thought that since he was with that little boy ... but he wasn't. Her stammering got worse. "I ... don't know. I ... I just thought ... I didn't think," she finished miserably. She looked at Bob. "But maybe if I could talk to him?"

"I can tell you his number all right," Bob said. "He works for the auction."

"He does?"

"Yup. Sits in the stands sometimes to make the bidding more lively."

"Oh, no," Paulie groaned. "Two of them forcing me up. I was probably the only one who really wanted Duke."

"Maybe," Bob drawled. "But if you hadn't taken him, Railway Three would have."

"How do you know?"

"Price of meat's up. Calves; pigs went real high. He'd have gotten his money back. Don't believe we've met," he said to Nana.

"Oh, sorry. Nana, this is Bob. Bob, this is my Nana, Mrs. Grace Horne."

"I'm happy to meet you, Mrs. Horne."

"Most people call me Nana, or Grace," Nana smiled. "I'm happy to meet you, too, Bob. I've heard a lot about you. Pink is very fond of you."

Paulie wished she had a hat, or a hood that would cover her entire head, face and neck. For an instant she wondered if her inability to keep from blushing was why her great-grandmother called her "Pink."

Bob grinned. "So, Brat, you said you called me. What can I do for you?"

Paulie didn't know what she would have said to Bob if he had been there when she phoned, or what she should say to him now. "I don't know," she answered. "I guess I wanted to ask if it would be possible to keep Duke at the stable until it gets torn down."

"Well, now, a few of the horses were sold privately. They'll be there for a day or two yet, and the developer fellows won't. Seeing as they've left me in charge of the shipping, I think we could find your horse a stall for a short while. Mind, it's just a few days."

Paulie was suddenly very tired. "Could I take him there now?"

"Got a halter?"

She pulled a braided twine rope from her jacket pocket.

"That'll do fine," Bob said. He reached through the fence and took it from her. Beside Duke he expertly made a knotted loop, through which he pulled a long loop that would go behind the horse's ears. The loose end of the rope was laid across Duke's nose, tucked under the far cheek-piece, looped behind his chin and brought back through the near cheek-piece. Enough loose end hung below the horse's cheek for the person leading the horse to have a decent lead line. "I'll take him back with me, and if he's lucky, throw him a handful of hay. Come mornin' he's your lookout."

Paulie wanted nothing more than to go home, but she knew Duke and Bob's history. Stepping on Bob's feet was Duke's specialty, and since his leg had gotten so bad Bob had no tolerance for Duke's games. The last time it had happened Bob had hauled off and kicked Duke in the shin so hard Bob had broken one of his toes and the horse was bruised for a week. Paulie was worried about both of them. "What if he steps on you?" she asked.

"He won't," Bob growled, glaring at Duke. "What horses remember best is what happened the last time they did something. As I recall, he wasn't too comfortable for awhile the last time he put his foot where it didn't belong. Come to think of it," he grinned, "neither was I."

Paulie was doubtful. "You sure?"

"I'm sure."

Paulie glanced at Nana, who stood quietly but was shivering. "Okay, then, I'll just say goodbye to him." She climbed through the rails and moved close, patting his neck. When she scratched his chin, he lifted it and flapped his lips like the Duke Paulie knew, the one who was continually chuckling at the world. It reminded her of his earlier behaviour. "Bob, you know when Duke was in the sales ring, he was so ... floppy. I'm afraid maybe he picked up something from a chestnut mare I saw today who looked really sick. Did you notice how funny he was acting?"

"Don't you worry about him, he's fit as a fiddle. He was just temporarily quieted."

"Bob, you didn't tranquillize him?" Paulie knew about the practice some horsemen had of sedating animals they either did or didn't want to sell to a particular buyer. If the buyer wanted a quiet mount and the horse was raunchy, the sedation quieted it. If the buyer wanted a fiery horse and the animal was a slug, the horseman would tell the buyer the horse was so fiery he'd had to sedate it to protect the buyer. If the horseman didn't want to sell to the particular buyer, he would sedate an already quiet horse to make it seem like breathing was an effort for it. "Tricks of the trade," Bob called them. At an auction it was illegal to sedate a horse unless it was done under the vet's orders, and then it was supposed to be declared to the bidding public.

"Old horse like this," Bob said. "Me and the vet figured it might be too hard on his heart to go through the circus without something to quiet his nerves."

"But it wasn't announced?"

"Sure it was. You recall how the auctioneer mentioned as how Duke had had vet attention."

She shook her head. She still had a lot to learn about auctions. She smacked Duke's shoulder with the flat of her hand, then reached up and tugged an ear. "You behave now," she whispered, giving him a final hug. "I'll see you tomorrow."

Nana, who had moved beside the fence, reached through and stroked Duke's nose. "He's a nice horse," she said.

Paulie's smile stretched. She still couldn't believe it. Duke was really hers.

As she and Nana were leaving, Paulie looked back to see Bob open the paddock gate and lead Duke through. He stepped ahead of the horse, reached over and picked up a gaff that lay leaning against the fence. "See this?" he warned. "You keep your clodhoppers where they belong. You got that?" Duke raised his near forefoot and took a step, placing his hoof back on the ground exactly beside Bob's boot and barely two inches away. Paulie turned, unable to watch; hoping they'd both make it back to the stable unscathed.

Nana had the taxi stop at Paulie's house first. Paulie hugged her. "Nana, thank you. I feel so ... I'm so lucky."

"I feel lucky, too, Pink. I had a wonderful day."

"Oh, Nana, did you really?"

"Really. It was just like when I was a little girl. I can't remember when I've had so much fun."

They hugged a second time and then the taxi was moving down the road and Paulie was on her way into the house. Now came her parents. What would they say when they found out what she'd done? She hadn't really expected it would happen. She'd wanted it to happen, but then she knew it wasn't going to, and then, suddenly, it had. At this moment she did not feel lucky at all. Oh, man, she was in big trouble!

— Seven —

Paulie detoured to the back door and let herself into the house quietly. She stopped on the landing, took her jacket off and hung it on a hook by the door, all the while hoping she could make it to the second floor and her bedroom without meeting anyone. She could hear someone in the kitchen doing something. Maybe their back would be to the kitchen door and she could creep past and up the stairs without them seeing her. Not to be.

Her mother saw her going past. "Hi," she said. "I didn't hear you come in."

Paulie spoke from the doorway. "Hi."

Her mother was kneading a large ball of bread dough. "Would you mind coming in here and greasing some of these pans for me?" she asked. "This is just about ready to cut into loaves."

Paulie gave up. She went to the sink and washed her hands. For several minutes she and her mother worked in silence.

"How did the auction go?" her mother finally asked.

It was Paulie's cue, but all she could get out was, "Okay."

Her mother glanced at her and continued. "You and Nana must have had quite a day. Grandma was a little worried. She called twice this afternoon to ask if you two were back yet. And she waited quite a while after dinner before she went home."

Paulie was annoyed. "Grandma doesn't need to worry about Nana. Nana's amazing. She knows all about auctions. She got right into it. At one point she stood up and … we had a wonderful time. Anyway, why does Grandma boss at Nana so much?"

"I know Grandma can sound gruff at times, but she loves Nana very much. She feels that all of her life Nana has taken good care of her and now it's her turn to take care of Nana."

"Does that include taking away Nana's gems?"

"Oh, Paulie, Grandma wouldn't take anything from Nana."

"Well, she did, because she wants Nana to move into the house with her and Nana doesn't want to."

"I can't say anything about that because I don't know anything about it, but I do know that Grandma would only have Nana's best interests at heart, whatever she did. If something happened that concerns you, Paulie, you should talk directly to Grandma about it."

Paulie knew the truth of that and was silenced.

Her mother's voice was gentle when she spoke again. "I'm glad you had a good time and that things went all right."

"Good grief," Gloria wrinkled her nose in disgust as she walked in from the dining room. "You stink!"

"So do you," Paulie shot back.

"I thought you said that barn you spend your time at was closing down."

"It is."

"So where were you, then?"

"None of your business, but if you must know, I was with Nana."

"Well, go outside and hose yourself off."

"You go hose yourself off, miss high and mighty!"

"Isn't there something pleasant you two could say to one another?" her mother broke in.

"I get tired of being told how much I smell," Paulie protested. "The way she goes on you'd think her nose was as long as Pinocchio's. Actually, it is, but ..."

"Paulie, that's enough."

"Okay, then, since I smell so bad I guess I'll leave."

In her room she sat on her pillow. She wouldn't thank her sister for it out loud, but this time Gloria's snootiness had saved her bacon because she'd given Paulie a reason to escape more questions. Still, Paulie knew, sooner or later Mom and Dad would have to be told about Duke. Below her, she heard Jerry's squeal and then his footsteps racing partway up the stairs and down again. Heavier footsteps followed his. "Again!" Jerry cried. "Do it again!" Gloria's husky laugh floated up the stairwell. Paulie wished she felt like laughing. A person should feel like laughing if they've just bought their own horse.

Maybe she should go back down now and at least get telling her mother over with. Her mother always said how calm making bread made her feel. Maybe she wouldn't get too mad. Maybe now that it was done neither of her parents would be really mad. After all, they always said how what was done, was done. And they'd gotten over other stuff — like the time she'd brought the rabbit home and it had had babies in the linen closet. And when she'd brought a ferret home and it had bitten Jerry's finger, then escaped under the fridge and it had taken her days to catch it. She sighed. A horse was not a rabbit or a ferret. She got up. She had to tell. She met Sam on the stairs.

"Where you been all day?" he asked. "I thought you were grounded."

"I got out for good behaviour."

"So where'd you go?"

"To the auction."

"Oh. Did your horse get chopped? Sorry. I mean did he ..."

"No, he didn't get anything."

"Oh. That's good. So where'd he ..."

"Shhhh." Paulie had heard her name. She listened and could hear her father talking to her mother in the kitchen. Although he was speaking in a low voice, he sounded angry. Paulie crept downward, moving closer to the portal.

"... that horse business," her father was saying.

Sam came down beside her and she put a finger to her lips.

"There are worse things she could be involved with," her mother said.

"Maybe, but she lets her imagination run away with her and she pulls crazy stunts. She's harder than all the others put together."

"Oh, I don't think so, but I agree we simply can't afford for her to have a horse right now. Maybe in a few years when Willie's…"

"In a pig's eye," her father butted in. "After Willie it'll be Gloria, and there are Sammy and Jerry to worry about, too, besides Paulie. All these bills, and with the recession and all the bankruptcies and layoffs there's not enough money coming into the store."

"I know," Paulie's mother said. "Well, let's be thankful they're all healthy and strong. I don't think we really have to worry about Paulie, Len. She's strong."

"Headstrong, in her case," her father said.

"That, too," her mother agreed.

Paulie turned back up the stairs. Sam started to follow. "I'm not good company right now, Sammy," Paulie said. She wasn't sure exactly what she'd heard, but two things were certain. Her father was mad at her about something, and he didn't like her. Until now, she'd had no idea how much he didn't like her. She'd never be able to tell him about Duke. She needed to be alone. "I'm just gonna go soak my headstrong little head," she told her brother and made herself laugh with him. Inside though, Paulie was not laughing.

In the bathroom she closed the door and locked it. She sat on the step stool and put her head in her hands. She felt like crying, but that, she told herself firmly, wouldn't solve a thing. She had a whole new problem. Now, besides finding a way to feed and house Duke, she was going to have to do it without her family knowing. Maybe not even Sam because if she told him he might give it away somehow. Nana had done all she could and Bob would be gone soon. Paulie was alone in this. Totally alone. She had no idea what to do. She sat until someone pounding on the door stirred her. "Go away," she snapped.

"Let me in!" Jerry demanded. "I'm supposed to have a bath!"

"I'm having a bath," Paulie said.

"No, you're not. I don't hear any water."

Paulie reached over and turned on the tub tap. She put the plug in the drain. "Do you hear it now?" A long, hot soak suddenly seemed like a very good idea.

"Mom!" Jerry yelled as he ran down the stairs.

Paulie stripped off her clothes and slid into the hot water. It was wonderful. She was just beginning to feel the muscles in her shoulders melting into weightlessness when the small fist hammered on the door again. "Mom says you're to get out of there," Jerry declared.

"Keep your shorts on," Paulie snapped. "I'm getting out in a minute."

"Mom said now."

"No, she didn't," Paulie said.

"Yes, she did. She said, tell your sister it's past your bedtime and ask her to let you in for a bath."

"That doesn't mean right this minute."

"Yes, it does. She said I could bath with you."

Paulie sighed. The toilet was in another room, which should mean a person could take a bath in peace, but there was only one bathtub in the whole house and that meant that whenever she was in the tub someone would come pounding on the door. She often bathed with Jerry, playing soap games and bubble games with him, but this was not one of the times she would enjoy it. "I'll be out in a minute and you can have the whole tub," she said.

"I'm telling," Jerry whined and she heard him going. Paulie sighed again, quickly scrubbed herself, climbed out and wrapped a towel around her body.

In the bedroom, Gloria was at her desk working. Paulie crawled into her bed and pulled her quilt over her head.

"What about your homework?" Gloria nagged.

Paulie didn't bother to answer. She was thinking. How, she wondered, was she going to keep a twelve-hundred pound horse a secret from her entire family?

— Eight —

"I owe you two weeks' wages and another two weeks for severance pay," Bob told her the next morning. Holiday pay on top of that." He handed her an envelope with her name on it. "Comes to $107.69 all told."

In the confusion of the past two days, Paulie had forgotten about the pay that was owed her for her job of cleaning stalls. It would buy feed. "Is there any hay I can buy?" she asked.

"I've got a couple of tons left. Fifty dollars a ton. You want all of it?"

Paulie thought. "Maybe not," she said carefully. "But if I decide I do, would it be okay to get it later?"

"Long as it's before the wrecking crew moves in. Day after tomorrow they'll be here to start levelling the place. If you let me know where to take the hay," he added, "I'll truck it for you."

She had read all the local ads for horse boarding. Only one farm she'd called had space available. The price was seventy-five dollars a month for a stall and a shared turnout paddock. Feeding and cleaning were not included. She would be responsible for those, unless she could work out some kind of co-operative arrangement with any of the other boarders, the owner had told her. "And of course," he'd said, "we'll need two references before we can consider you." Paulie had told him she would call back.

"I'm working on finding a place," she told Bob. "I'll have to let you know."

"Fine."

Bob watched her walk away. At the stable, kids had come and kids had gone. Paulie had stuck it out for three years without a horse of her own to hold her there. He knew what kept bringing her back week after week. She had that tainted blood — blood that was as much animal as it was human. It made her comfortable around horses, dogs, birds, bulls, probably even alligators if it came to it. He'd seen her kind once or twice before. She could talk to animals in a language that had little to do with words. Animals understood her. But her ability got her into trouble in the human world — alienated her from her own kind. She had not yet learned to control the animal side; could not cover up the emotions that rose and fell in her with their hot, red flow. She had not learned, either, to blanket the honesty of her emotions with the fog of denial and lies. Still, though he knew what drove her and sometimes saw the pain it caused her, he had never invited her to share her problems with him. And she had never tried to share them uninvited, or pried into his private affairs.

He turned back to his task of loading bunkhouse furniture he had lived with for ten years into the truck. He was to deliver it to the mining company that had bought it. In a few days all his stuff would have to be cleared out.

Paulie took Duke's old bridle from where it hung beside the stall door. "Get over," she ordered when the horse crowded her against the side wall as she came up beside him. Duke stayed where he was and Paulie put an elbow into his ribs and pushed. He took a step sideways. "That's better," she said, moving to his head. She slipped the bit between his teeth and put the headstall over his ears. When she'd first started bridling him, it had sometimes taken her upwards of half an hour to get the bit into his mouth. With time, he had quit tossing his head like a sock tumbling in a dryer, but it could still be dicey trying to get a bridle on him. She was grateful today was not one of those days. She had exactly an hour and a half before school started. That meant only half an hour to ride. She led him out and swung herself onto his back. Immediately he started to prance. She dug in her heels and yelled, "Okay, go!" Duke jumped into a run.

When they passed Bob, he hollered, "Slow that horse down! You wanna tie him up?"

Paulie sat up straight, squeezed her fingers into fists to hold his head and closed her legs against his sides to force him forward till his mouth bumped against the bit and he slowed down to a trot. There was so little time and

Duke so wanted to go, but she knew better than to run a horse before it was properly warmed up. She'd seen horses pull up in agony when their back end muscles tied themselves in knots because they ran too hard too soon. That was particularly true for old horses. Duke strained against the bit, but she forced herself to hold him in.

They headed west, going toward the city, following the edges of fields that had been baked hard by the summer sun and were now frozen with fall frost. Sun-spots bounced and glittered off the grass and frozen dew. At the second field she let him go. His hind legs reached and gathered, his front legs reached and stretched. The distance of his strides grew until he was in the four-beat gallop of a race horse. At the end of the field he jumped the ditch and Paulie turned him north on a long, straight dirt road. Duke lowered his head and stretched his neck, gathering even more speed. Paulie's hands were soft and followed his mouth; her body moved in perfect time with his. He was a free, wild thing, racing a herd of sun-spun stallions that barely touched the ground across the prairie with a speck of a girl upon his back. The wind whistled around her, cut into her cheeks, turned her earlobes and her nose red.

When they had gone about five kilometres down the dirt road, Paulie turned him and slowed him. He came down roughly, dancing a jig, tossing his head, refusing to settle. "Come on boy, quiet down," she crooned, patting his neck. Sometimes he had more energy than she did. If he was old, she thought, she wanted to have known him when he was young. She lectured him. "We have to go home now and you have to cool down or Bob'll give us both what for." She knew the sharpness of Bob's tongue when a horse was brought back to its stall still foamy with sweat. Not without a fight, Duke relaxed. Finally he dropped his head and began to swing his back in an easy, flat-footed walk. Paulie dropped the reins on his neck, letting them dangle in long, loose loops. Sitting totally relaxed with her own back swinging to match the horse's stride, she looked around.

They'd been on this road many times. It was an eight-kilometre strip that ran inland from the highway, slicing through wheat, rape and canola fields, providing access for the farm machinery. There was only one house, set back from the road down a long, gravelled driveway. Closer to the road was a market stand with the words "Charms Market Garden: Fresh Produce" stencilled in metre-high letters on its slanted roof. In the summers, when Paulie had been starting or finishing a long ride, she sometimes stopped at the stand and bought apples and other fruit. It was closed up now. As they passed it she gazed at the boarded-up building and at the fenced area behind it where the husks and stalks of harvested vegetables remained. There were about four fenced acres, Paulie judged, and an obvious thought struck her.

This would be a good place for Duke. The more she thought about it, the better the idea seemed. The owners weren't using it now and wouldn't be for the winter months — not until next April or May would the stall open again. She could offer them Duke's manure, which she would carefully collect and pile in any spot they chose, the same way Bob had taught her to pile the manure from the stable to allow it to compost for good fertilizer. She could offer herself, too. She could weed, or plant, or work in the stand, or anything. It was a perfect barter. She would have a home for Duke; they would have fertilizer and free help. She picked up the reins and nudged Duke to a faster pace. They cantered down the driveway toward the house.

When she got close to the house she discovered it looked deserted. Some windows had curtains pulled tightly together; some were boarded. Across the front steps a massive spiderweb stretched from column to column of the porch structure, as if put there to guard the entrance. Paulie rode around to the back. The double doors of the garage were down and on the door of a shed there was a padlock. A derelict car was rusting beside two garbage bins that were overflowing. Refuse littered the ground. Paulie dismounted, ground-tied Duke by dropping his reins on the ground and telling him, "You're tied," and went up the back steps and knocked on the door. No one answered. Disappointed, she mounted and rode back to the barn at a slow canter, hoping Bob would know the owners of the place. But Bob was nowhere to be found.

She put Duke in his stall, fed him and checked his water. There was no time left to groom him. "I'll give you time to roll and brush you for half an hour tomorrow," she promised, and then grumbled, "I'd do it tonight but I can't because I'm grounded." Because she had always been the earliest riser in the house and was usually out somewhere doing something by the time the others got up, no one ever questioned her morning whereabouts anymore. But it was different in the evenings. Duke, whose nose was buried in hay, kept right on munching, unconcerned.

Paulie pedalled as fast as she could but, once again, she was late for school. She had to go to the office for an admittance slip. "Detentions are in the library tonight," the secretary told her as Paulie signed the late book.

"I can't stay after school today," she blurted.

"Reason?" the secretary asked.

"I ... just have to go home."

"I'll need to confirm that with your mother."

"No," Paulie said. "Um ... I mean, couldn't I come in early tomorrow morning instead?"

The secretary put down her pen. "You know the rules, Paulie. We don't do detentions in the morning and if you can't serve a detention on the day of the offence, we have to confirm it."

"Well, I'd do something ugly like clean the bathroòms or pick up garbage, or something?" Paulie tried. The secretary's eyebrows rose. Paulie sighed. "My dad has already grounded me this week, and if I get another detention right now I'll be grounded for life. Locked in a time warp with no way in or out — forever." She twisted her face and rolled her eyes as she said the last.

Lowering her head to hide her smile, the secretary said, "I doubt it's as bad as all that. But I'll let you do something disgusting, just this once. You can spend your lunch hour today cleaning gum off the bottoms of desks, and first thing tomorrow morning bring me a garbage bag full of trash you've picked up from the school grounds."

Paulie thanked her and went to class.

Throughout the day she was distracted. In social studies, when her teacher asked her to name the place on Earth considered to have the highest standard of living and give the reasons it was considered thus, she was busy dreaming about painting the market-garden building. In her mind the tall, stilted green lettering was transforming to long red sweeps outlined with purple that read *Duke's Barn*. When her teacher repeated the question, Paulie murmured, "Charms." The class giggled. Her teacher was not amused. She assigned Paulie a mini-essay on the importance of paying attention and said she expected it on her desk the following morning. The whole day went like that.

"Where are you going?" Jenny asked when they met at the lockers after the last class. "It's volleyball tryouts."

Paulie slipped her backpack on. "That's today?"

"Yeah, and you're coming."

"I can't," Paulie said. "I'm grounded."

"Man," Jenny moaned, "what did you do now?"

"It's a long story."

"Well, get out of it. Grovel. Tell them you'll serve your time another time."

Paulie shook her head. "I already did that and it starts today. There's no chance my dad'll let me out of it. But there's another...never mind, go," she said when she saw that Jenny was looking at her watch and bouncing on the balls of her feet.

Jenny slammed her locker shut. "Okay. I've heard this guy is a stickler for time. He makes you run a kilometre if you're late and I've got about one minute to get changed. I'll call you tonight. Oh, I guess I can't because you're grounded."

"Phone calls are okay," Paulie said.

"Really? To my mom being grounded is the same thing as being buried. No anything allowed," Jenny complained. She ran down the hall toward the gym and the change rooms yelling, "Call you! Be there!"

Paulie wondered if there was any adult in the world who wasn't a "stickler for time," as Jenny put it, and where her friend thought she might be if not at home when she was grounded.

She was quiet through supper. After supper she asked her father who owned the market garden. "I don't know, honey," he answered. "Why?"

The "why" caught her off guard. "Uh, nothing really. Just something to do with a socials project. ...It's out of town, on the corner of the highway and Cooper Road. Do you know the place I mean, Mom?"

Her mother shook her head. "No, but it might be listed in the Yellow Pages of the phone book under garden centres or food products or produce. Often an ad for a business will give the name of the proprietor."

Paulie hadn't thought about using the telephone book. "Thanks," she said. "I'll look."

She set the phone and the telephone book on the table in the breakfast nook and settled onto the bench. There was no listing for the market garden in the Yellow Pages. She turned to the White Pages, looked up "Charm," and groaned. It was an unusual name, but there were eighteen of them, none with an address on Cooper Road. *Well*, she decided, *I guess I just have to start at the top and call them all if I have to*. She got through about half a dozen of them before other members of the family began to nag her to get off the phone. Reluctantly she gave it up for short periods, but when the others were talking she stayed close, annoying them. Her father chased her away with, "Pauline, it's very rude to hang about when someone else is on the phone." She retreated just far enough away to see when he came out of the kitchen. Then she went to the phone in the basement family room and took up where she'd left off.

The twelfth person she called said his uncle had been connected with the market garden, but that branch of the family had long since moved away and he did not know who owned the old place now. None of the other Charms in the book knew anything about the market garden.

At nine o'clock, Paulie put the receiver back in its cradle and stretched herself out on the couch. Her homework could wait, she thought. Perfect, who had been asleep on her lap, stretched herself out on Paulie's belly and settled back into a purring sleep. Intending to come up with a new plan of attack, Paulie fell asleep instead.

It was midnight when her father shook her awake, his hand gentle on her shoulder. Perfect was gone. Her father helped her to her feet and followed her as she stumbled up the stairs. At the door to her room he kissed her on the top of her head and left her.

At 4:30 a.m. a distant bell pinged her out of a sound sleep. She groaned, pulled her arm from under her pillow, and shut off the alarm on her wristwatch. Pressing warmly against the small of her back she felt a ball of fur. Perfect always liked it best under the covers.

Paulie was used to getting up early, but even for her it was an effort to drag herself out of bed at half past four, and in her dopey state an even greater effort was required to move quietly enough not to wake her sister. She tiptoed to the bathroom, where she brushed her hair and teeth, and then downstairs. Not daring to turn on a light, she felt her way through the house to the kitchen. She opened the fridge. Apples and cheese would do for breakfast. For good measure, she took a long swig from the milk carton. She wrapped the cheese and, on the landing by the back door, put it and the apples into one of the big pockets of an old winter jacket of Willie's she had claimed for her own. She pulled on her boots.

It was the middle of the night outside. Paulie headed for College Avenue, a well-lit, main thoroughfare that connected with the highway leading to the stable. There wasn't much traffic. Occasionally a car or truck passed her. Once in a while huge trucks pulling trailers loaded with goods they were freighting rumbled eastward. The noise of them and the wind they created were unnerving. When they passed her, Paulie crowded the very edge of the road.

When she turned off the highway, there were no more street lights. There was only her bike light that shone a pale yellow triangular swath into the blackness ahead. Paulie pulled the zipper of her jacket up to her throat and reached into one of her pockets for a wool toque she was glad was there. As well as being extremely dark, it was cold.

The glow of light that flooded the barn when she flipped the switch by the door warmed her. Duke whinnied. The sound of it echoing off the walls of the stalls and corridors made Paulie realize he was the only horse still here. It was a sad realization somehow, a feeling of the end of something important to her. He whickered softly when she opened his door to drop hay into his feeder. She rubbed his nose. She leaned against him, patting and scratching behind his ears and the poll of his head; listening to him. She inhaled the rich, musky smell of his flesh. For an hour she let him eat, brushing every hair on his body until it gleamed, and then she led him outside and across the parking lot to a small paddock. While he rolled on the ground, tossing his big, muscular body from side to side and flailing his legs in ecstasy, she mucked out his stall.

She had shovelled out all the manure and almost completed loading in fresh sawdust when she heard footsteps coming down the alleyway. Paulie recognized Bob's uneven walk. He came to the stall door. "Thought you might be here," he greeted her.

"I thought you said that when you no longer had to play nursemaid to a bunch of ornery nags you were going to stay in bed till noon," she teased. "What happened to your vow?"

"I'm gonna do that — soon's that gaggle of geese in the south field gets gone. Those suckers make as much racket as a dozen trains clacking over steel rails or a houseful of gossips. And they're right under my damn window."

"Well, I'm glad you're up," she declared, "because I won't be here at noon and I need to know something. Do you know who owns 'Charms Market Garden' — or when the owners will be back?"

"Owners now are the developers. That place has been bought up by them same as this place. Same as all the land around here."

Her face fell. "Oh. Are they going to tear down the buildings?"

"Far as I know they're flattening everything in sight. Got plans for building what amounts to a whole new mini-city out here. I heard some of their plans have been kiboshed because some of the land is still zoned agricultural, which means they can't build on it, but it never takes any developer long to convince council the taxes they can get from streets, houses and businesses are worth way more than for agricultural land."

Paulie felt a glimmer of renewed hope. "If Charms' is a market garden, would it be zoned agricultural?"

"Hard to say. The people who decide what land is zoned as what have some funny ideas about what's suitable for farmland and what isn't."

"Do you know how I could get in touch with the developers?" she asked.

Bob knew exactly where she was headed. He didn't want her to get her hopes too high. "Those fellas think on a scale as wide as a budget line," he said. "The only thing that matters is profit and loss. Chances are they won't jump at the chance to have a horse and a kid on their property."

"Well, maybe I can convince them I'm a profit," Paulie returned. Her jaw was at its most stubborn and her brown eyes flashed.

Bob's eyes crinkled. "They'll be around about seven-thirty or so tomorrow."

"Good," Paulie said. "Will you be here?"

"Yup." He hesitated. "The wrecking crew starts work about eight."

Paulie stopped working, stepped out of the stall and closed the door. She looked at him. "That early?"

He nodded. "They'll expect all the horses to be gone when they get here."

"Oh, Bob."

He squatted, looking for a suitable chewing straw. "I'm sorry, Brat. I wish there was something I could do." He stood up. "I'll load your hay into the trailer this morning. Tomorrow morning Duke can go in, too. Temporarily. He can't live in there."

"I know," Paulie said. "Is it all right if I leave him in the paddock today and tonight? He likes it outside."

"He should go in tonight. You've been pampering him with that blanket and he hasn't got a snow coat yet."

"Oh, then I'll have to put him in now."

He waved her away. "Come dark, I'll bring him in. Aren't you gonna be late for school?"

Paulie jumped. It was 7:15. She got her bike from where it leaned against a wall. She would just have time to make it to school and pick up garbage before classes began.

At 8:27, puffing, she set a plastic garbage bag on the counter in the outer office. "Is this enough?" she asked the secretary.

The secretary smiled. "Yes."

"So I can go to class?"

The secretary nodded and Paulie was gone. She deviated to the washroom to wash off garbage and horse; slid into her desk in the math room just after the final buzzer sounded. Jenny whispered from behind her, "I called and called but your phone was busy all night. Did you get your homework done?"

Paulie shook her head.

"Rats," Jenny muttered, "neither did I. Did you study for the socials quiz?"

Paulie smacked her forehead with the palm of her hand. It wasn't the quiz that bothered her. The worst she could do was fail that. She had forgotten all about the essay on listening and her socials teacher did not accept excuses, ever. She was toast. She opened her math book to a blank page and started writing.

"Pauline!" she heard her name spoken in an exasperated tone. She looked up. "The answer to problem 4a, if you'd be so kind."

"I don't know," she mumbled.

The teacher was moving toward her. "And is that what you are so diligently working on?" He was beside her now and she stared up at him, willing him away. Her arm moved so that it partially shielded her book.

He wasn't moving. He was waiting for an answer. "It's ... socials," she finally confessed. He reached down and picked up her book.

"Ah," he said after examining it for what seemed forever, "lucky Miss Brewster. How, I wonder, does she get you to work so hard?"

The class tittered.

He began to read aloud what Paulie had scribbled:

Sometimes I don't pay attention and then my dad and some of my teachers think I'm deaf. But I'm not. Even when I'm not thinking about it I can hear my alarm go off in the morning and my sister's breathing and my heart beating after I've ridden my bike a long way. Sometimes I hear the quiet, too, and then I stop and listen to it because it's not really totally quiet. There are always sounds just beyond my knowing what they are. Maybe grass or leaves rustling like silk skirts moving in the wind. Maybe snowflakes plonking onto bare branches of trees or evergreen needles. Which brings up the colour green and in the past minute even though I wasn't really listening I heard Mr. Green get mad twice.

The class broke up, one or two of its members laughing so hard tears ran down their cheeks. Paulie kept her eyes on her desktop. With considerable dignity, Mr. Green replaced her notebook on her desk and walked back to the front of the room. "Well, Paulie," he said from beside his desk, "are you listening now?"

Paulie nodded.

"Please add pages forty-three, forty-four, forty-five and forty-seven to your homework tonight. And tell Miss Brewster I wish her luck."

It took five minutes for the class to quiet back down and Paulie knew it would take weeks, maybe months, for them to let her forget it. She considered never returning to school.

Before Paulie could say anything to Jenny after class, they were caught up by the other two girls who formed the group of four they usually hung with. Melodie was flapping a piece of paper and burst forth with the news that a boy had passed her a note asking her to go with him to the Welcome Back Dance next Saturday night. Jenny squealed with delight. Paulie had noticed a couple of boys — after all, there were a lot more of them in six classes of grade sevens than there had been in one class of grade sixes — but she couldn't quite latch onto the excitement. Maybe that was because she had brothers. It didn't matter what she thought, though, because Melodie was talking so fast no one else needed to say a thing. It was the last class she had with Jenny and she didn't see her after school. Volleyball practice, she knew, was at least three times a week.

When she phoned Jenny after supper Jenny's mom said, "No, Paulie, she just left with Melodie to go to *Hot Chick*. They'll probably be there to pick you up in a few minutes."

"I'm not going," Paulie said.

"Oh. Well, Jenny will be back about half past nine. But isn't it you who was saying how funny that movie is?"

"I, uh, yeah, I think it would be funny," Paulie said.

"But you're not going?"

"No," Paulie said. "I'm grounded."

"Oh, that's too bad. I'll let Jenny know you called, but I won't tell her to call you back then," Jenny's mother said.

Oh jeez, Paulie thought, remembering too late what Jenny had said about her mother's policy on grounding. Paulie didn't think Jenny had been grounded more than maybe twice in her whole life. At least not in the nine years Paulie had known her. Jenny was one of those people everyone called "mellow." She went with the flow, easily fitting into anything going on around her. It was the reason she was the conduit through which all the friendships in their group flowed. It was Jenny who plugged them all into one another. Paulie knew that and she was not usually jealous of time Jenny spent with any of the others, or anyone else, but still, she wished she could have gone to the movie she had indeed thought would be hilarious. But she couldn't, and by the time Jenny got back she would probably be asleep. Four-thirty came awfully early. "I'm allowed to talk on the phone," she told Jenny's mother, "but I'll probably be in bed when she gets home. Don't bother to tell her I called. I'll talk to her tomorrow."

"All right, Paulie. Bye bye," Jenny's mother said.

Paulie spent the evening doing math.

— Nine —

By the time Paulie made it to the barn
Wednesday morning, she was soaked
from the slushy rain. She changed into the
jeans and windbreaker she kept stuffed in the rubber pail
with Duke's brushes and hoof pick, and hung her school
clothes over a stall door to dry. She'd stick to the indoor
arena this morning, she decided. It was too wet outside and
anyway she wanted to be right here when the developers
came. She gave Duke a quick brushing and saddled him.

Riding him proved difficult. When she wanted him to
canter, he kept breaking to a walk. When she lengthened the
reins to encourage him to stretch his neck and relax, he crow-
hopped into a gallop. When she asked him to shoulder-in,
he bent his body almost in half and ignored her outside leg,
swinging his hindquarters off the track so that he ended up
travelling sideways across the arena. Finally, he laid his ears
flat against his head and bucked hard twice, almost unseat-
ing her. Paulie brought him to an abrupt halt.

"What is wrong with you this morning?" she demanded. He, of course, did not come up with an answer. Maybe it was her. Her mind wasn't exactly on what she was doing. Where were the developers? For that matter, where was Bob? She had left the big end door open, but she hadn't seen anyone drive into the parking lot that separated the arena from the covered bays where horse trailers and the machinery for the day-to-day operation of the stable used to be parked. Now, only one four-horse trailer remained. Beyond that was the office building. Duke bucked again and she decided enough was enough. She'd pack up hers and Duke's stuff and take it to the trailer. Maybe Bob was loading hay into it like he said he would or something. She got off her horse and led him to his stall.

Except for the one horse trailer, there was nothing and no one in the bays. The flat-bed trailer Bob used to haul feed was gone. So were the forklift, the tractor with its implements and the stone boats. She opened a small door at the front of the horse trailer, threw her gear inside the tack room, and climbed in to stow it. When she'd done that, she opened another door. The feed room between the tack room and the four stalls that made up the main body of the trailer had been filled with hay.

The back end of the trailer faced a wide grassy area that separated the parking lot from the paddocks. When Paulie checked it, she saw that the doors were open and the ramp was down, as if Bob had gotten it ready to load Duke in.

Attached to the bay farthest away from the trailer was a small shop where Bob made things, including hand-forged shoes for every horse in the barn. Maybe, Paulie thought, he was there. He wasn't. There was a lock on the door and she could see through a window that the shop, too, had been emptied of tools. She looked over at the office. No lights on there. Maybe, she thought, he was actually sleeping in like he'd always said he wanted to do. If so, she hoped he'd wake up soon because it was already getting light and her watch said 7:19. She went and knocked on the door of the office. No one came. She could wait until a little after 7:30 but then she needed to get going to school.

Bob had said Duke was to be loaded into the trailer this morning. She'd seen him load horses into trailers, but she'd never done it herself. Should she try it without him? If she left Duke in his stall, would Bob get back before the wreckers came? She had a growing feeling she should not leave here without at least knowing where Bob was. *Maybe I didn't knock hard enough*, she told herself. *Maybe he's really sound asleep because the geese are gone.*

She pounded on the door. Still no answer. With a feeling of shame mixed with fear, she tried to look through a window to the right of the door. Partially closed, slatted blinds blocked her view. At the side of the building there was another window a little higher up the wall. If she climbed on the skirting bar, she could reach it. Should she? She knew this window would look into the bunkhouse — Bob's bedroom. What if he was there and he was asleep? Then she'd be like a peeping Tom. She stayed where she was and knocked more loudly. The minutes passed.

At last she turned the handle and pushed. The door was not locked. She put her head inside. "Bob? Hello! ... Heelllo! ... Is anybody here?" There was no answer. She stepped in. Against the rising day she could see that this room, too, had been cleaned out. Only the woodstove and the built-in table Bob had used for an office desk remained. The chairs, file cabinets, horsehair couch, even the double sink, were gone. At the far end of the room, off to the right, were two closed doors. Behind one was the bathroom; the other led to the bunkhouse. Calling, she walked slowly across the room to the bunkhouse door. She should not be doing this, she thought. It was wrong. But everything seemed wrong. Bob's collection of *The Far Side* comic strips should be on the wall above the table, where they'd always been. His personal saddle should be hanging on the peg that stuck out from the wall opposite the desk. The wood box should be full of wood, waiting for the coldness of November before Bob would use a stick of it to keep himself warm. She knocked on the door to his room and, when there was no answer, opened it.

The room was empty. A feeling she wouldn't have described as relief, but was, made her shoulders droop. She didn't know what she'd expected. Where was he? Somewhere outside where she hadn't seen him? Her sense of intrusion overtook her. She whirled and retreated to the trailer, ashamed at what she had done. In her family, no one ever opened the closed door to another person's bedroom without permission.

But where was he? In Paulie's experience, he had never not been there when he had said he would. He wouldn't have forgotten about Duke, and about her, would he? She swallowed. No, he wouldn't. He just wouldn't. But it was half-past seven now. What was she supposed to do now? She supposed she would have to go ahead and load the horse. It should only take five minutes or so to do that and then she could leave.

Forty-five minutes later she stood at the top of the trailer ramp, shaking. Duke was at the bottom, leaning back, tightening the rope tied to his halter a little bit more. His toes were dug into the grass. His front legs were angled and stiff. His chin was up, and his thick neck was locked in a stand-off, the muscles bulging. After he had pulled loose twice, Paulie had wrapped the rope around the metal framework of one of the trailer stalls, but she hadn't tied it. Bob had told her stories of balking horses bending steel posts as easily as she crushed aluminium pop cans with her hands. Once, he said, he'd seen a horse take an entire set of stock racks with him when he decided to jump out of the back of the truck. Miraculously, the horse had not been hurt. The truck and racks, however, had been trashed. So Paulie had simply looped the rope around the bar for support and held onto the end with all her might.

Her own legs were stiffly locked; toes pushed against the lip of a cross-rung. She did not lean backward, but her arms were bent, also locked, and her biceps and other muscles bulged like the muscles of Duke's neck. There was no give in her hands. She was angry. Duke didn't seem to care that the halter had tightened so hard behind his ears and against his cheeks that she was sure the circulation in his head was being cut off. Nor did he care that her hands were burned raw from his sudden back jumps after he had advanced a few steps up the ramp. He didn't care that her right shin had been badly bruised when she'd hit the steel frame of the doors after one particularly hard lurch he'd given, either. "Fine," she said. "Stand there like a bullhead and cut off your own circulation. I'm not giving you one inch." Bob said a human could never win a physical fight with a thousand-pound horse, but she was willing to try.

As if responding to her voice, Duke stopped leaning back and straightened up on his legs. The rope slackened and Paulie felt the shock of release all the way up her arms into her shoulders and neck. She flexed her hands. Instantly Duke jumped backward. When she felt it going, she clutched frantically at the rope. It seared through her palms and fingers, unravelled from the post and flew out of the trailer and down the ramp to follow the retreating horse like a snake slithering through the grass. Duke trotted to the fence line of a paddock, lowered his head, and started eating. Paulie stood staring in disbelief. Her hands were filled with hot knives. Tears streamed down her face. A few minutes later, Bob pulled his truck into the parking space beside the office.

Paulie couldn't see the driveway from the back of the trailer. She had not seen Bob drive in, but she heard the door of his truck close. *The truck*, she thought. *I didn't connect that his truck was missing.* But for all she knew it might not be Bob's truck door she heard. Maybe it was the developers or the wrecking crew. Whoever it was, she didn't want them to see her like this. She turned into the trailer, trying to pull herself together. She wiped her face with the bottom of her jacket. "Got a horse here who seems to be missing an owner," Bob's voice chided as he led Duke toward the trailer.

Paulie took a deep breath and turned. "You were gone," she accused.

His eyes took in her face, and her hands. "Guess you didn't get my note," he said softly.

"What note?"

"The one saying I wouldn't be here. I left it pinned to the door of Duke's stall."

"Oh. No, I didn't see it."

"I guess you were worried."

She touched one flaming hand to the other. "Sort of."

"Well, you've got a reprieve."

"What's that?"

"The developers have been temporarily stopped by a cease and desist order. A group of people who want to save these parts as agricultural land got a court order forcing things to stop before they got started."

"You mean the stable won't be torn down? You'll be staying!"

"Now hold your horses. Like I said, the order is temporary. The developers still intend to go ahead, if not today, tomorrow. All it means for us is that Duke can stay in his stall for another day. 'Course by now you might think even a dog food can's too good for him."

Paulie looked at the horse standing peacefully at Bob's side. "I couldn't load him," she said.

"He's an ornery old cuss. What say we try again now? We don't want him having any more horse laughs on us."

Paulie wasn't sure. Her hands hurt and she was so late for school that when she did get there they'd probably lock her in the principal's office until sometime after Christmas. She'd also have some pretty tall explaining to do, so really, she thought, there was no hurry to get there at all. She shrugged.

"Okay then, here we go." Before Duke could react, Bob flipped a loop of rope behind his rump and ran the loose end through the halter under his chin. "Which way did he go when he backed off?" Bob asked Paulie.

"Mostly to his left," she said.

"You come down and stand on that side of the ramp. That will discourage him from going that way."

Bob took a firm hold of the end of the rope, turned and limped confidently up the ramp. Duke willingly followed until he got to the edge of the wood, where he abruptly braked. Before the horse got halfway into his backward lean, Bob gave his end of the rope a sharp yank and continued walking. Duke jumped away from the surprise of pressure behind his buttocks, took two tentative steps forward, and stopped. Again Bob gave the rope a yank. It was confusing for the horse. Something was biting into his back end, but there was no one there; nothing to kick at.

His only course of action to escape it was to move forward, away from it.

It took three more starts, stops and sharp yanks before the horse followed Bob all the way up the ramp and into the back of the trailer, where he stood white-eyed and splay-legged, snorting. Still holding his end of the rope firmly, Bob reached for a cross-tie that was bolted to a beam on one side of the trailer and clipped a short-shanked lead to the cheek-piece ring of Duke's halter that was closest to that side. Crooning to the horse and stroking his nose now, he reached for a second cross-tie and clipped it to the other cheek-piece ring. Duke was secured. Paulie was amazed. "How did you do that?" she wanted to know.

"Horses have pea-sized brains," he said. "They can't figure out what's happening in two directions at once; so if you've got their attention in front and they can't *see* anything behind them, a little rope bite will convince 'em they've been kissed by a ghost and they want to get away from that sucker pronto so they come on forward."

Paulie laughed despite herself. "Good trick."

"Yeah. We'll give him some feed and leave him there for awhile so's he can think things over. Feed a horse in a trailer and they'll decide it ain't such a bad place to be."

"And then?" Paulie asked.

"It's your call. Like I said, you've probably got an extra day at best."

"I have a letter I was going to give to the developers when I saw them this morning, but they didn't come. Could you give me their address so I can send it to them?"

"I'll be seeing them this afternoon. I can deliver your letter."

"Would you read it for me?" she asked. "I want to make sure I've included everything and I also wanted to ask if it's all right for me to use your name for a reference."

A shy pride, as if he'd never been asked that before, crept into his voice. "Yup on both counts."

She got her pack from the trailer tack room and, using her sore hands gingerly, took the letter out of it. Bob noticed the blood that had run from her palms between her fingers and caked the backs of her hands.

He took the letter and read:

Dear Mr. Developers,

My name is Paulie and I have a horse named Duke. I'm looking for a home for him and would like to ask if he could live in the market garden if you are not going to tear it down. I could pay by supplying fertilizer for the garden and working there on weekends and in the summer. I don't know very much about gardens but I am a willing learner and a good worker. P.S. Duke would be moved someplace else whenever you wanted to start the garden. For a reference for me please contact Mr. Bob Stewart.

You can phone me at 528-8936 or tell Bob if it would be all right for me to keep Duke at your market garden. I hope it's all right.

Signed, Paulie Burke

Bob folded the letter and carefully put it in a pocket inside his jacket. "Looks just fine," he said. He motioned toward the truck. "I reckon we can do something about those hands now. There's a kit in the truck." He poured Mercurochrome into her palms and over her fingers, then expertly bandaged them. The figure-eights he made with the tensor bandages he put over the gauze reminded Paulie of the leg wraps she'd seen him do on horses. The wrappings were about as thick. She'd never be able to hide the fact that her hands were hurt.

"Can't we make the bandages smaller?" she asked.

"Nope. And don't you take them off till your mother has a look at those," he ordered.

Her mother. Oh, lord. What was she going to tell her mother? She'd have to make up something. That was bad enough, but she'd just gotten off grounding and now it would begin all over because she was late, again, for school. She could skip, but the school had a policy about phoning students' homes and confirming illness if a student was missing for more than half a day. There was no way out. She had to go to school and then she would have to go home.

— Ten —

At school the bandages saved her. The secretary didn't need a note to see that Paulie was injured and she assumed the injury was the reason Paulie was late. She tore off an admittance slip and signed it, asking Paulie what she had done to her hands.

"Nothing much," Paulie said. "Rope burns."

Mrs. Monahan winced. "Ouch." She gave the slip to Paulie. "You'd better take good care of them so they don't get infected."

"I will," Paulie assured her.

She went to English, the final class before lunch. When she opened the classroom door and closed it using the heels of her hands as best she could because she could no longer stand to have anything touch her palms, the teacher smiled sympathetically at her. He told her where they were in the lesson. "Don't try to write if you don't want to," he said. "Just listen. You can get the notes later."

She sat in the vacant desk across the aisle from Jenny, who promptly leaned over and whispered, "What's going on?"

"Nothing."

"Nothing? You've got your hands bandaged up like that and nothing's going on?"

The teacher looked in their direction.

"I'll tell you later," Paulie whispered.

Jenny wrote her a note. *Meet me at the lockers after class.*

Reaching across to deliver a reply saying she would meet her friend, Paulie's eye caught another classmate holding his nose and staring in her direction. Across from him another boy was smirking. Great, she thought. She'd forgotten to change from her riding jeans and windbreaker back into her school clothes and she smelled strongly of horse and probably of sweat from fighting with Duke. Her clothes were still sitting in the tack room of the trailer. She would have to go back and get them.

A bell signalling the end of class made Paulie jump. She'd almost fallen asleep. Students began to move from their desks to the door and Paulie rushed into their midst. Jenny's voice calling her name stopped her.

"I can't talk now," Paulie mouthed to her friend.

"What? Are you saying you're not going to meet me?" Jenny yelled, waving Paulie's note at her.

Paulie pushed through a couple of kids to get closer to her friend. "I'm sorry, Jenny," she said, "but I just remembered I have to go somewhere right now."

"Somewhere where?"

"To the stable. I was in such a hurry to get here I forgot

to change out of my barn clothes. I've gotta go back and get my school clothes and change before our next class."

"Yeah," Jenny said. "You are definitely not dressed too cool and you are a little, shall we say, high. Is that where you were this morning? I thought the stable was closed down."

"It is."

"So what were you doing there? What happened to your hands?"

Paulie needed an ally and Jenny was her best friend. But Jenny was afraid of horses. She had tried to be brave when Paulie had taken her to the barn a couple of times, but she'd ended up leaving before Paulie could persuade her to get on a horse. And she'd claimed loudly that she couldn't understand why a perfectly rational person would want to spend time picking muck out of horses' feet, brushing botfly eggs off them or, much worse, shovelling poop out of stalls. All Paulie would accomplish by trying to explain this morning to Jenny would be to launch an avalanche of questions and defences for what she was doing. She didn't have time for that now.

With the lengthening silence, Jenny complained, "You know, you've never been what I'd call real yappy, but you used to at least talk to me. Lately, trying to talk to you is like talking to my pet guppy. Are you mad at me or something?"

"No," was all Paulie said.

The look of complaint turned to one of hurt. "I don't care. If you don't want to tell me, don't then."

"Jenny, I'm not mad at you. There's just a lot going on and I really am in a hurry."

"You're always in a hurry. You never have time to do anything anymore. We're supposed to be friends."

This was hardly fair. It had been Jenny who had been in a hurry, or out, the two times Paulie had tried to talk to her in the past few days. But it was true there was a distance growing between them. Paulie had spent a lot of time this summer and fall at the stable, and this past week ... she hadn't made time for anything but Duke. She felt bad. Still, if she told Jenny everything, what could Jenny do? What she *would* do, probably, was deride Paulie for getting into trouble again. The last thing Paulie wanted was that. "I have to go because if I don't I'll be late getting back to the first class after lunch and Mrs. Monahan will crucify me," she said.

"Are you coming to the dance on Saturday?" Jenny asked.

Paulie sighed. "I don't think so."

"Okay then, see you around," Jenny said in a dismissive kind of voice that made Paulie very sad.

"Next week ..." she began, but then stopped. Next week what?

Jenny gave her a look she couldn't read. "Whatever," she said.

Paulie hurried to the main door of the school and disappeared through it on the run.

— Eleven —

At the stable, Bob was outside the office talking to two men who were dressed in raincoats and new-looking, wide-brimmed, cowboy hats — the kind Bob said politicians wore when they were trying to get the rural vote. Paulie recognized one of the two as the man who had frightened Duke. The other was a tall man she had never seen before. She detoured from the trailer and went to them. As she approached the men, they stopped talking.

"Are you the developers?" she asked directly.

The tall man nodded curtly.

"Did you see my letter?"

"Are you Paulie Burke?" the same man asked.

"Yes."

"Then we saw your letter, and I have to tell you we can't allow you to take your horse to the market garden. The demolition crew should already be there and when they finish there, they'll be here."

"What happened to the cease and desist order?" she demanded.

The man who had frightened Duke laughed; the other man silenced him with a look. "It's been appealed and overturned for that parcel," he replied. There was an awkward silence. "Bob has asked us to let you keep Duke here," the man said, "but we can't do that either. We expect the decision on this land to come down tomorrow and so you'll have to have your horse out of here by then."

"Oh," was all Paulie could manage before she turned away. She did not stop at the trailer but walked to the barn, where no one would see her. She picked up a pail and carried it to the aisle beside Duke's stall. Turning the pail over, she sat. She was tired, scared, sore, and fresh out of ideas. She stared at the floor, seeing nothing.

Bob's hand on her shoulder startled her. "You've given it a good run," he said, "but maybe it's time to take Duke back to the auction and let him take his chances. Things could be different this time."

A dry sob escaped Paulie's throat. "No!" she said, "I'm not giving up. Ever."

Bob rubbed his chin and was quiet for awhile before he said, "Well, I admire your spunk. But you still gotta come up with someplace to put this horse and his feed."

The only place Paulie could think of was Grandma's house. She couldn't take Duke there, that was for sure, but there were buildings on the property besides the house. Maybe she could at least put the hay there. As for Duke ... at her house, in the backyard, there was an old shed. She had already thought about using it and had classified the idea as dumb, but she was desperate. It was too small to house both the hay and Duke, but it would hold Duke. Nana had said keeping farm animals in city limits was illegal. So Duke would have to temporarily be classified as a domestic pet. How was she going to do all that? Another sob threatened to escape but she swallowed it back. One step at a time, she reminded herself. She'd start with the hay. "Is there a phone where I could call some-one?" she asked Bob, who was leaning against the stall wall, waiting.

"Phone in the office has been cut off, but there's a cellu-lar in the truck you can use," he said.

She jumped off the pail and ran to the truck. She dialled Nana's number.

"Eight-two-eight six-zero-four-five."

"Grandma, this is Paulie. Can I talk to Nana?"

"I'm sorry, Pauline, Nana's napping right now. I'm on my way out the door, but if you like I'll write a note for her."

"Well I ... will Nana be at home this afternoon?"

"Yes. Is there a message you'd like to leave?" her grand-mother prodded.

"No, no message. I'll call her back a little later."

"Fine, but give her at least half an hour before you try again, will you," her grandmother said. "Goodbye, dear." There was an audible click and a dial tone sounded in Paulie's ear.

Paulie hung up. She couldn't wait another half hour. This might be the only opportunity she would get.

"I couldn't get through to Nana," she told Bob, "but Grandma said Nana's home and I think if we take the hay to her house we can put it in a building there. We couldn't take all of it, though. Would it be all right if I just bought maybe twenty bales? I can buy more hay someplace else when I have a proper place for it."

"So you want us to truck the hay and Duke to your Nana's?"

"No, not Duke. I'll come back with you and get him. He's not going to the same place. I want to ride him where he's going."

"You're not gonna go lookin' for more trouble, are you?"

"What I'm looking for is to stay out of trouble."

He laughed.

"Can we take my bike with us when we take the hay?" she asked.

"No problem." He tossed her a pair of leather gloves. "Think you can help load with those hands?" he asked.

"Yup," she answered.

She put her fingers under the twine to lift a bale of hay out of the trailer feed room, and gasped with the pain. Bob saw, said nothing, and bent his back into loading the truck. To each one of Paulie's bales, he loaded five. When they'd secured the load, he drove it and Paulie to Nana's house. While Paulie walked up the front walk and along the side of the house to the solarium door, Bob drove the truck around to the alley and parked by Nana's back gate. Paulie saw Nana sitting in a chair in the solarium reading a book. Without knocking, she went in.

"Hello, dear," Nana smiled. "I got a message you telephoned and here you are. Would you like some tea, or some juice and cookies?"

"No thanks, Nana. I don't have very much time. Um, could you come outside?"

"Of course, dear, I'll just get my galoshes."

Paulie waited while Nana disappeared into her room and then returned. She was wearing her coat and her bedroom slippers. She reached for the door, but Paulie stopped her.

"Nana, you've got your slippers on," Paulie said.

"Oh, I wonder where my galoshes would be?"

"In the closet?" Paulie suggested. Nana turned a complete circle and looked again at Paulie. Her eyes were vacant. Paulie knew there were things Nana forgot, like people's names sometimes or some detail she was trying to remember about a story she was telling. Paulie forgot those kinds of things, too. And sometimes Nana forgot where she had put something. But never before had Paulie seen her great-grandmother's eyes look totally lost, as they did now. It made Paulie feel like she couldn't catch her breath. "Nana, sit down. I'll get your boots for you."

As suddenly as Nana had been lost, she seemed to find herself. "Thank you, dear," she said. "I'm afraid my head sometimes gets a little fuzzy."

Paulie opened the entry closet and took out Nana's boots. She waited while Nana sat and put them on. "Are you okay now?" she asked before Nana stood up again.

"Fine," her great-grandmother said.

When they were outside, Nana took a deep breath of the cold air. "Ah," she said, "I love the beginning of winter, don't you, Pink? Look, it's starting to snow."

It was true. Tiny flakes of dry snow were drifting earthward from the sky. Winter was not Paulie's favourite season, but today this early first snowfall was welcome. "Nana," she said, "I've got a problem."

"Do you, Pink?"

"Yes. I have some hay and I have to have a place to keep it. It would just be for a little while, until I find someplace permanent, but I have to move it right now because the stable is being torn down. Could I use the greenhouse, do you think?"

Nana looked across the yard to the large fibreglass greenhouse. "I think that would be all right, dear. I'm not sure what's in there anymore. I do most of my gardening inside now, in the solarium."

"Can we look?"

"Of course."

When they opened the door to the greenhouse, Paulie said, "Oh." The interior was almost completely taken up with a large trestle table loaded with ceramic pots and bowls and jugs. Boxes of more of the same filled the space under the table as well.

"Oh, yes," Nana said, "I'd forgotten. Dorothy's taken to storing some of her work out here."

"Is there another place we could put the hay?" Paulie asked, looking around the yard. The only other outbuilding was the double garage beside the house and that, Paulie knew, was where her grandmother parked her car and kept her yard tools. There was the yard itself, but they couldn't keep the hay in the open where it would be seen by her grandmother, not to mention ruined by the weather. Feeling miserable, Paulie answered her own question. "There is nowhere else," she said out loud.

"We can put it in my room," Nana said brightly. "There's plenty of space. It will be like I'm sleeping in a barn. Or I could move into the big house the way Dorothy wants me to. If I did that, you would have an entire room for your hay and Dorothy would be very happy."

"But you wouldn't," Paulie said. "You'd hate it."

"Oh, I don't think I'd hate it, dear, but I am very comfortable back here. Is there a lot of hay?"

"No, only twenty bales."

"Well, that's settled, then. We'll put it in my room and I'll stay, too."

Paulie beamed. "Bob's already parked the truck in the alley by the back gate. Could we bring the hay in through that door?" She pointed to a door in the end of the house nearest where they stood. "Then we wouldn't have to take it through the solarium."

"That's a good idea," Nana agreed. "Would that nice young Bob like to come in for a cup of tea, do you suppose?"

Paulie had never thought of Bob as young and she was pretty sure he wouldn't have described himself that way, either. She smiled. "He probably would, Nana, but we really can't. I still have to get back to the barn and move Duke."

"Of course you do. I'll just go and make sure everything's out of the way of that door."

"Great."

Nana bustled off while Paulie went to tell Bob they could start unloading.

"Think you can build the bottom rows of a proper stack, Brat?" he teased her as they each carried a bale through the gate.

The bales weighed almost eighty pounds. Paulie only huffed in response. The back door to Nana's part of the house opened and Paulie and Bob walked in. Paulie was shocked. Where there had been antique carved chests, curved-legged tables, stacking tables inlaid with mother-of-pearl, Nana's large comfortable rocking chair where Paulie had sat on her great-grandmother's knee listening to stories — there was now empty space. The twenty-by-twenty-four-foot room contained only a bed, a small chest of drawers with Nana's hotplate on top, one straight-backed chair, and a small rocker.

"Wow!" Paulie said. "You've moved almost everything out. It's so … empty."

"Dorothy's been cleaning again," Nana said sadly. "She was afraid I might trip on something and hurt myself."

"Nana, I hope to have someplace else to put the hay in a couple of days, but what if Grandma comes in to clean some more before then and she sees it? She'll flip."

"Oh, I believe she's finished in here for awhile," Nana said. "Our usual cleaning day is Tuesday. I'll just lock my door until then and that will be all right, won't it."

Paulie felt vaguely disturbed. "Are you sure?"

"It is my room," Nana said. "Dorothy doesn't need to know everything, does she."

Paulie was happy to agree. "Nope. And you're sure right about one thing, there's plenty of room for you and the hay."

In less than fifteen minutes she and Bob had moved and stacked all the bales. Looking at the wisps of hay that telegraphed a path from the truck to the house, Paulie was glad the snowflakes were getting thicker. The path was being covered. She unloaded her bike and put it against the house. "I'll be back tonight to get my bike and some hay, Nana," she said.

As she and Bob drove away in the truck, Nana waved.

— Twelve —

Duke wandered aimlessly around a large paddock nosing the light covering of snow that now lay upon the ground. A blanket of white fluff covered the ridge of his back and when he raised his head, his muzzle and whiskers were white, too. "Sorta looks like he's been into the ice cream and forgot to lick his lips," Bob commented. He chewed on a piece of hay and leaned his elbows on the fence. "I'm gonna miss the old fart."

Paulie turned her face away. "Are you going to like it up north, Bob?"

"Can't tell for sure," he answered. "Haven't been there yet. But I never went anyplace I didn't expect to like."

Paulie's voice was small when she spoke again. "Do you have to go?"

Bob removed the straw from his mouth. "Well now, I don't guess I have to do anything. There's a pretty piece of land right here I've got my eye on, but buyin' land takes money and saving money is one thing I haven't been too good at. North is where the work is. From what I hear, the big ranches up there are beggin' for experienced cowboys looking for good money. That's me."

To her surprise and his, Paulie slid her arms around him and buried her face in his shirt front. "I don't want you to go," she said.

To his knowledge, Bob had never been cried over before. He didn't know what to do. "Here now," he said, "there's no call to go and do that. You and I have been friends, haven't we?"

Paulie nodded.

"Well, friends want for one another to keep seeing new things. Movin' and seein' things kinda keeps the old blood pumping 'cause when a person quits being interested in new things, he's dead, or he might as well be."

He unwound her arms and, pushing her back, leaned down until they were eye to eye. "Friends smile when a friend moves on and wish him high times. Even ol' Duke is smilin'. Look at his silly white grin. There you go, now that's a pretty memory for me to take with me. Where are you gonna take that old cayuse to?"

"I don't think I should tell you," she said.

"Why not?"

"Because I want you to think I'm staying out of trouble."

"Aren't you?"

"I hope so."

He laughed. "I'm gonna miss you," he said.

She had to look at the ground when she said, "I'm gonna miss you, too." She squared her shoulders. "The wheelbarrow and forks and shovels are still in the barn. Should I put them in the tack room in the trailer when I take mine and Duke's stuff out?" she asked.

"I'll be here a day or so yet. I'll load 'em up when I deliver the trailer over to the auction."

Paulie lifted a bandaged palm into the air, saying, "High five." He raised a large leathery hand and she hit it with surprising strength. "High times," she said, and slipped sedately through the fence, where she collected Duke and led him toward the barn. She'd brush him off with some hay and let him dry a little more while she got her stuff from the trailer. Duke's brushes, her binder-twine rope and assorted other things would fit into her backpack. She'd put his bridle on over his halter and they'd be on their way.

— Thirteen —

It was four o'clock when Paulie rode Duke into the city. School had been out for half an hour. For the whole ride she'd been thinking about how she was going to get Duke into the shed in her backyard without being seen and how she was going to keep him there without anyone knowing. A horse left certain signs around, not the least of which was manure in large quantities. The closer she got to her house, the riskier it all seemed. She was four blocks from home when a disturbing sound caused her to halt. Gloria's laugh. She'd know it anywhere. It was as loud and as sharp as a horse's whinny.

Paulie looked around, searching her surroundings for cover. There wasn't much. Spindly trees lining the boulevard, houses built almost side by side with only cement sidewalks and sometimes a narrow strip of grass and a low fence separating one from the next. The new church. Maybe she could hide on the other side of the building. She spurred Duke into the parking lot and around a corner. She got off.

Keeping Duke behind her, she peered out into the street. Gloria and a bunch of her friends were walking up the sidewalk across the road. Half a block away one of them angled, stepped off the sidewalk into the road and began to jaywalk to the church side of the street. Paulie knew that taking a shortcut through the church lot was a popular route to her dad's store. She looked behind herself. She couldn't make a break for it. She'd be seen no matter which direction she rode. And if she tried to lead Duke around the far side of the building she'd run into trouble with the new landscaping that was roped off there. There was a side door a little way away. She'd just read the story of the Von Trapps, a family that had escaped from Austria before the Second World War and became famous singers. When they were escaping, they sought sanctuary in a church.

Frantically, Paulie pulled Duke toward the door in the building, opened it and led him in. As soon as the door closed, she remembered the snow outside. Duke's hoofprints were all over the place! She opened the door a crack and peeked out. No one in sight, but she could hear the girls coming closer. They sounded just like the geese Bob had complained about. A gaggle of gossipy girls. Paulie couldn't risk going out there. She prayed they'd be so busy gossiping they wouldn't see the hoofprints.

She and Duke were in an alcove. On the right there was an open coat room and stairs going down to the basement. Paulie saw several coats and jackets on hangers in the coat room. On the left three steps led up to the rectory. Dead ahead was a wide door that opened into the church proper.

The door was closed, but voices could be heard through it. Someone was talking. Then it was quiet. Paulie scratched Duke's neck and whispered to him that he was being such a good boy. And then, an organ burst sent Duke reeling and fifty voices began to peal "Nearer My God to Thee."

Paulie hung onto Duke's bridle and hoarsely pleaded with him to stand still. His hooves clattered on the ceramic tile. His tail lifted. He dumped a pile on the shining floor. Paulie groaned. The music played on. She had to get out. She opened the door, looked, and pulled the jittery horse outside. Grabbing hold of his mane and bridle with one hand she shortened the near-side rein so that his head was pulled sideways into his body. With her other hand she took hold of his wither. She swung herself onto his back. Duke wheeled into the bridle, turning in circles until Paulie straightened his head and he took off across the lot and down the alley in the opposite direction to that which Gloria and her friends, who had not come through the church lot after all, had gone.

At the end of the block Paulie pulled the horse up and scanned the street. There was no traffic. She turned right and galloped him toward an entrance to the city park that was two blocks from her own house. She was glad this was a residential area. Traffic was usually light except for a flurry of activity between five-thirty and six-thirty p.m., when people were arriving home from work. Only one car passed her.

Framing the road into the park were thick, clipped caragana hedges. Behind the hedge on the left there was a stand of oaks, a large group of spreading junipers and other plants she didn't know the names of. A horse could be hidden in there. Paulie tied Duke to a low branch of an oak tree. Satisfied he would be hard to spot from any direction by anyone who didn't know he was there, she went to scout out her backyard.

Entering cautiously through the back gate, she could see the snow in the yard had not been disturbed. She crossed quickly to the shed. The ten-by-fourteen-foot building had no windows. It was dark inside. She stepped in and closed the door behind her. She flipped a switch and the single bulb that hung from the ceiling in the middle of the room lit. She hadn't been in here for a long time. There was so much junk! It took several minutes for her eyes to adjust to the dusty, shadowy interior and for her mind to sort out how she would make room in here for a horse.

At the far end, running the full width of the building, was a workbench on which sat several cans of nails, screws, hooks, wires, bolts, locks, door handles, paintbrushes, paint trays and other assorted bits and pieces her father thought would "come in handy sometime." She could put all that stuff into the cardboard boxes that had been thrown on top of the old cans of paint that cluttered the shelf under the bench. In the middle of the floor there was a jumble of bikes but those, Paulie knew, belonged on the bike hooks her father had mounted on the side wall. On the same wall he had also put up several hooks for the shovels, rakes and garden forks that now leaned, along with an old curling broom, against one end of the workbench.

The cross-country skis that lay along the base of the opposite side wall could go on the overhead rafters. The rototiller would fit into the corner beside the boxes she would stack there, and there would be plenty of room for Duke on the other side of the room. She could tie him to the bench and use the top of it for a feeder for him. She would have to bring water in a pail.

She worked quickly. When she had finished the cleaning, she filled a bucket with water from an outside tap and put it on the floor near the workbench. She went to fetch Duke. He was standing quietly, dozing on three legs.

When she returned, there were still only her footprints denting the snow in her backyard, and they were rapidly disappearing under a new layer of flakes. Her luck was holding. She led Duke to the shed and held him at the door, letting him have a good look. His eyes widened until they were rimmed with white and his skin quivered when she touched it. He snorted, and pawed, but he didn't pull back or try to run away. Paulie was grateful. In a low, lilting voice, she coaxed him inside. He followed her, turning his head this way and that to stare at the hanging shapes. When she tied him to the workbench, he sniffed its top and then, apparently accepting the lodging, lowered his head to drink from the pail. Paulie rubbed his forehead. "I know where there's a bag of oatmeal. I bet you'd like some oats. And right after supper, I'll get you some hay. I know this isn't very big but you'll be safe here. No one comes in here from now till April. Well, they won't if you're quiet. You have to be very quiet, okay? I'll take you out as much as I can. Just please be quiet and don't get scared. I'll take good care of you." He raised his head and she kissed his dripping muzzle.

Outside it was dark but she took the curling broom and swept all the hoofprints she could see from the yard and the alley; then went to the house. At the back door, she took several deep breaths. So far, so good. She opened the door and listened. She could hear the television playing in the family room. The rest of the house seemed quiet. She closed the door softly. There was nothing cooking on the stove and no one in the kitchen. She got a bag of oatmeal from the pantry and took it outside. Opening it with her penknife, she poured a quarter of the contents onto the counter under Duke's nose; then put the bag into one of the boxes in the back corner. She returned to the house.

No one stopped her on her way to her room and Gloria wasn't there. She couldn't believe her luck. She tossed her backpack on her bed and pulled clean clothes from her drawers.

In the bathroom she took off Bob's bandages, showered and got dressed again. It was hard. The hot water had hurt her hands horribly and it was getting harder and harder to straighten her fingers. Her hands were curled into a sort of baseball mitt shape. She wanted to leave them like that, but she couldn't. She had to use them as normally as possible. What did her mother do for burns? Ointment. She opened the drawers of the vanity looking for supplies and found Ozonol, sterile gauze squares, tape and scissors. Trying to remember how Bob had taught her to wrap horses' legs and tails, she did the best she could. At least the tape is thinner than the tensors, she told herself when she was finished. Now if I just put some gloves on. She found a pair of white cotton ones in the Tickle Trunk in a storage cupboard — costume gloves for Minnie Mouse — and a pair of black stretchy ones in her underwear drawer in her dresser. The white ones would be too conspicuous. The black gloves had leather insets in the fingers and on the palms. She'd bought them long ago when she'd begun assembling the riding outfit she intended to wear in horse shows someday. They would do. She pulled them on. Exhausted, she lay down on her bed for a ten-minute nap. Almost instantly she fell asleep.

Fifteen minutes later, her eyes popped open. It was after six o'clock. She arrived in the dining room just as her mother was setting a bowl of mashed potatoes on the table beside a bowl of turnips. All afternoon Paulie's mind had been occupied with Duke. Now it was school that loomed large in her thoughts. Had they phoned this afternoon to ask why she was absent? From under her brows she glanced at her father and her mother. Neither of them looked mad. She pulled out a chair and sat, surprised she was one of the first at the table. "Where is everybody?" she asked.

"Gloria's out for dinner and Sam's at basketball," her mother answered.

"Sammy's gonna teach me how to play basketball, he said so," Jerry put in.

Paulie wanted to ask why everyone else got to stay out at suppertime when she had to be home, but she knew better. Her father's decree regarding her had only come down after she had "forgotten" to appear for dinner a few times without phoning. Anyway, it was just as well the others weren't here. She wouldn't have to worry about whether or not they knew she'd missed school this afternoon. She helped herself to stir-fried vegetables with tofu, potatoes and turnips. No one spoke until her mother asked her, "What kind of a day did you have, dear?"

Paulie visibly relaxed. The school hadn't phoned, or if they had, her mother hadn't been home to receive the call. Most likely, Paulie thought, Mrs. Monahan hadn't made the call. She'd seen Paulie's bandaged hands. She might think Paulie had gone home because of them. However it had transpired, her relief was genuine. "It was okay," she replied.

"How come you got gloves on?" Jerry said.

Paulie tried to hide her hands inside her sweatshirt sleeves.

"You really don't need to wear gloves at the supper table," her mother said.

"I do. I'm doing a ... cream treatment on my hands. I have to leave the gloves on for a couple of days, maybe longer."

"Doesn't sound healthy to me," her father said.

"Yes, it is. It's very healthy," Paulie begged her mother with her eyes.

Her mother softened. "It's probably all right to do your treatment for one night, but by tomorrow I think you'd better take them off. Your hands need air." She looked at her daughter. "You're looking very tired and a bit pale, Paulie. Do you feel well?"

"I feel fine."

"Are you sure? Let me feel your head."

Paulie leaned forward and her mother touched her forehead and cheeks with the back of her hand. "You don't feel as if you have a fever."

"I don't," Paulie repeated. "I told you I'm fine."

"Did you hear that vandals dumped a load of manure in the church during choir practice this afternoon?" her father said.

Paulie nearly spat out her mouthful of potatoes and turnips.

"Where did you hear a thing like that?" Paulie's mother said.

"From Ed. He was in the store buying the paper and he said someone went into the church when the choir was practising and dumped a load of manure all over the floor of the side entry. A couple of them said they'd heard some sort of racket but no one paid any attention to it. It took them awhile to clean the place up and air it out. Ed says it'll probably smell for days."

"Why would anyone do something like that?" Paulie's mother asked.

"Ed figures it's because the church is supporting the low-income housing development."

Paulie's mother shook her head. "I don't understand why some people are so afraid of giving others a decent place to live."

"You know what we've run up against ourselves, Kris. People are afraid the neighbourhood will change, turn bad."

"It'll be the same neighbourhood it's always been. Why can't those people believe that if we just treat the new families with the same friendship we all used to treat one another with, the new people will be friendly back and we'll all benefit."

"Some would say you are being idealistic."

"May I be excused?" Paulie asked. "It's not my night for dishes."

"You hardly ate a bite," her mother said.

"I want to go, too," Jerry said.

"Right after you eat the broccoli you've put under the edge of your plate," his father said.

"Aw, Paulie didn't eat that much broccoli."

"She didn't pick her broccoli out of her stir-fry and hide it under her plate," his father said. "The rule is, what you take, you eat."

Paulie left the table with her brother and her father fighting over broccoli. She headed for her grandmother's house.

At her grandmother's, Paulie let herself in the front door with her key and called hello. Nana and Grandma were eating their supper at the table in the kitchen. Paulie told them not to get up. "I just came to get my bike," she said. Nana asked her if she'd like a piece of chocolate cake. Paulie loved chocolate cake but if she took it she would have to take off a glove to eat it. She said no, thank you.

Her grandmother went to the counter and cut and wrapped a piece, which she handed to Paulie. "You're looking a little peaked," she said. "Are you feeling all right?"

"I'm feeling fine," Paulie said.

"You're not losing weight, are you? These days so many girls your age are too thin. Girls your age ought to have meat on them. You need a little fat to have the proper calcium for your bones and teeth, you know."

Paulie put the cake in her pocket and looked down at herself. "I'll never be too thin," she said ruefully. There were times she wished her body was like Jenny's. She was as tall as Jenny, but where Jenny had a slender, ethereal shape that Paulie thought of as "regal," Paulie had the broad shoulders and solidity of a football player. She knew she moved more gracefully and had more endurance than Jenny had, but it was Jenny who got the calf-eyed looks from the boys. Not that Paulie'd be interested in anyone who looked at her like a moony calf, she told herself, but ... She pulled herself back to the present. Duke would be hungry. "Is it all right if I go through your room, Nana?"

"Of course, Pink," Nana smiled. "I'll come along and let you in."

Paulie caught the pained glance her grandmother shot toward Nana, and the unease Paulie had felt about the locked room earlier returned. As she stood waiting while Nana fished her key out of a pocket in her dress and unlocked the door to her room, the full weight of the look Paulie had seen on her grandmother's face dropped into the pit of her stomach like a bowling ball. She would have to get her hay out of here as soon as she could, that was for sure.

A whole bale was too much for her to carry. She cut the strings of a bale with her penknife and took out one-third. She retied the twine around the rest and took her twine rope out of her pack to tie up her loose flakes. So that she would not leave a trail of hay behind her, she had also brought a black plastic garbage bag. "Maybe I should come and get the rest of this bale tonight," she said to Nana as she put the hay into the bag, "then I won't have to come tomorrow morning. Would it be all right if I came back tonight?" She moved to the door she and Bob had used. "I'll come to this door so I won't have to go through the house, and I'll let myself in with my key so you won't have to come next time."

"Your key won't work in this lock, dear. When this room was added to the house, the locks put on the doors were different from those on the main house. There is only my key for them, so I'll leave this door unlocked until I go to bed. How would that be?"

Paulie knew her grandmother went to bed early. "Fine," she said. "I'll try to come back right away." She kissed and hugged Nana before she exited.

She had no difficulty strapping her load onto the ratchet behind the seat of her bike and soon got the hang of how to balance it as she pedalled home. She put the hay on the bench in front of Duke and made another trip to her grandmother's, this time more confident and taking the rest of the bale. She stashed it in a box and put that box on top of the other boxes at the back of the shed; then settled in to spend some time with her horse.

While he ate his hay, she ate her cake. Later she cleaned up the manure he had already dropped by putting it into the garbage bag. She'd use garbage bags to collect all the manure, she decided. Maybe in the spring she could even sell it to gardeners, the way the manure at the stable had always been sold. Of course, she'd have to find someplace to store all those bags in the meantime, but she'd figure that out later.

When she returned to the house, she discovered her grandmother was in the living room talking to her parents. She could hear her voice from the kitchen. "... call the doctor tomorrow and take her to see him no matter what she says," her grandmother was saying.

"Has anything happened that would upset her?" Paulie's mother asked. "I mean, anything that would make her feel she had to lock her room?"

"I have been taking her things out of it bit by bit," her grandmother admitted. "I want her to move into the house. I'm so afraid she's going to have a fall or hurt herself out there and I won't even hear her. Her eyesight is not what it used to be and she has these blank spells."

"She's so independent," Paulie's mother said. "Maybe she'd feel better if you just let it be for awhile?"

Her grandmother was indignant. "She's acting so strangely lately, I can't let it be. Someone has to make sure she's all right and that she hasn't left a burner turned on on that infernal hotplate of hers. I've been after her to give that up for months but she won't hear of it. I'm afraid she's lost touch with reality. If she doesn't open her door tomorrow and let me into that room, I'm going to call a locksmith, and I'm definitely taking her to a doctor."

Paulie's father sighed. "Is everyone out of control?"

Paulie didn't wait to hear any more. She went swiftly out the back door and biked to her grandmother's house.

The back door to Nana's room was locked. Nana was in bed. Paulie kept knocking and calling, "Nana, it's me, Paulie," until her great-grandmother finally opened the door. "Thank goodness," Paulie said as she rushed inside. "Nana, Grandma's at our house. She's mad at you for locking your door on her and she's talking about calling a doctor and a locksmith and ..." Paulie hesitated. "Oh Nana, everything is going wrong. I've gotten you into so much trouble."

"Goodness!" Nana replied. She patted Paulie's hand. "You're not to worry, child." A sadness came into her eyes. "I'm sorry to have upset Dorothy. In the excitement I quite forgot myself. But you mustn't think you've done me any harm, Pink. I'm quite capable of getting myself into difficulty. When I was a girl, people used to say my middle name was Trouble."

Paulie stared at her. "That's what some people call me."

Nana smiled. "Well, now that we're in it, we'll have to go about fixing it, won't we."

"How?"

"We'll tell Dorothy all about it and she won't have any need to worry anymore."

"We can't!" Paulie protested. "If we do, my parents will find out about Duke and he'll be killed!"

"Oh, I don't believe you'd have to worry about that, dear. Both your mother and your father are very fond of animals. When he was a boy, your father had a horse of his own."

"You don't understand," Paulie protested.

"Perhaps not."

Nana seemed to be waiting for her to explain. Paulie didn't know what to tell her. Everything was a mess. "I'll take care of it," she said at last. "I'll talk to my dad."

"I think that would be best," Nana said.

Paulie gave her a hug. "I have to go, Nana."

"All right, Pink. Now don't you worry, everything will be all right."

Paulie wished she could believe that. But she didn't.

The adults were still talking, but that didn't stop her. She walked in and with no preamble she confronted her father, interrupting the conversation that was going on. "Dad, did you have a horse when you were little?"

Her father was annoyed. It took a minute before he answered. "That was a long time ago."

"But you did, right?"

"Paulie, you are being very discourteous."

"Nana said you loved animals," Paulie insisted.

"Whether or not I like animals or had a horse are not subjects I'm prepared to discuss with you right now. Your grandmother, your mother and I were talking, and you have very rudely interrupted us. It's quarter to ten. Definitely past your bedtime. I want you to go upstairs now. If you have something you want to discuss, we'll talk about it tomorrow. Goodnight."

"Mom ..." Paulie pleaded.

"Your father's right, Paulie, you are interrupting. Goodnight, honey."

"Goodnight, dear," her grandmother said. Paulie was barely able to respond, "Goodnight," before she turned and left the room.

In the bathroom she tipped bubble bath under the faucet, eased herself into the foaming swirl, and let the water come up almost to the tub's rim so she could float. She thought how nice it would be to just sink into a watery world. All would be blissful oblivion. She sank under the suds, holding only her hands clear of the wet. She held her breath, but eventually came up. There were no answers to anything, she thought; then thought she was too tired to think. She'd let it all go down the drain. She pushed the plug lever down with her toe and sat and watched the whirlpool of the water leave the suds behind.

Gloria was home now; once again at her desk. "What, you've gotten so smart you don't have to open your books anymore," she said when Paulie pulled her pyjamas off her bed and put them on. "Or could it be you've quit school altogether and plan to be a bum? Don't you dare drop that wet towel on the floor."

Paulie could see the speculation in her sister's eyes. So Gloria knew she hadn't been at school that afternoon and hadn't passed it on. That was a switch. For a moment she wondered if she should try to talk to Gloria, at least about Grandma and Nana. Gloria loved Nana, too, Paulie knew she did, and she had more experience with Grandma than Paulie did. Then Gloria's eyes landed on her gloved hands and a smirk erased the speculation.

"Aren't those your riding gloves? You planning to pretend your bed is a horse and practise being a jockey like National Velvet? I've a news flash for you — you'll never ride in the Grand National, sport."

Paulie didn't bother to retort. She got into bed and pulled up the covers, rolled over, and closed her eyes, but her revived worries bubbled in her mind and kept her awake. She'd told Nana she'd take care of it and she hadn't; not at all. So what would Grandma do to Nana? And what about Duke? She was more certain than ever that if her father found out about Duke he would send the horse directly to the cannery. Tomorrow was Thursday. She had no idea what she was going to do, but she'd have to miss another day of school, that was certain. What could they do to her for that? Nothing compared to what was going to happen to Duke. It was almost dawn before she drifted into sleep.

— Fourteen —

Something hard landed on Paulie's stomach. It stayed there, then it wiggled. It was heavy. It pulled at her hand and the pain dragged her up, up, out of her sleep. "Come on!" Jerry cried. "I have to show you something!"

She opened her eyes. He had on his snowsuit and his boots. His boots were on the wrong feet. His excitement set her on edge. "Be quiet," she rasped. She looked across the room as the lump of blankets that was Gloria became a head and blankets.

Gloria looked at the clock that was on the table beside her bed and moaned. "Get out of here right now, Jerry, or I'll throw a shoe at you. I've got at least forty minutes left to sleep."

"There's a creature in the toolshed!" Jerry burst out.

"Oh, God," Gloria groaned, "he's been watching *E.T.* again. Shut up, Jerry and get out of here!"

Paulie rolled off her bed and grabbed some clothes. "Come on," she said to Jerry, "you can tell me about it downstairs. But you have to be quiet or you'll wake everybody in the house up and they'll all be mad." In the kitchen she pulled a pair of jeans and a sweater on over her pyjamas. Jerry started to speak, but she put a finger to her lips to silence him. "Not yet," she cautioned.

"I found a horse," he whispered.

Paulie's head ached. How was she going to get out of this? She put on her jacket and boots and took Jerry out into a world covered with a cotton-ball carpet. She stopped. It was so beautiful. So quiet! All night it had snowed and the huge, fluffy flakes were still coming down. The world glowed with a ghostly light. Jerry had run ahead of her. "Come on!" he yelled. She got to the door of the shed just as he was walking under Duke's belly. "Look at my horse," he said. "Isn't he beautiful!"

"Get out of there," she ordered.

Jerry ignored her.

For the sakes of both the horse and boy, Paulie controlled her fury and tried to speak in a calm voice. "Jerry, get out from under that horse right now. Walk out here." When he didn't, she reached for his arm and pulled him out to her. Holding him with a vicelike grip she explained, still trying to keep her voice calm, "Duke weighs half a ton. If he stepped on you, he'd squash you like a bug."

"Ow! You're hurting me. Let me go right now or I'll kick you one!"

"Only if you promise you'll stay right here beside me and not move anywhere else."

"Awright awready. Let go!" She did and he rubbed his wrists. "The horse won't step on me, he likes me," Jerry said. "And his name's not Duke, it's Roger. I finded him and I cut his hair."

Paulie's head jerked toward the horse. In spite of the commotion Duke was standing quietly, but something about him was different. His eyes seemed to be far more prominent than they had been and his nose looked longer than ever. That, she realized with a shock, was because his forelock had been cut in a crooked line not far below his ears. Instead of a forelock he had bangs. Paulie stared at Jerry.

"What?" Jerry said. "His hair was in his eyes. Mommy always says it's not good for a person to go around with hair in his eyes."

Paulie spotted a pair of scissors lying on the bench and wanted to scream. She picked up the scissors. Still trying to control the level of her voice, she said, "You could have put out one of his eyes with these," she said.

Jerry defended himself. "I wouldn't of. He liked it. He did, too! He stood real still the whole time. He likes me. I'll show you." Without warning he moved behind the horse and grabbed his tail.

He gasped when Paulie's hands snatched him. She lifted him off his feet, carried him to the corner of the workbench farthest from Duke and slammed his buttocks down on its top. "He could kick your head in with one swipe of his leg."

Jerry started to cry. "He wouldn't," he sobbed. As if to prove Jerry's point, Duke moved closer to where Jerry sat and stretched his muzzle as if to put his chin in Jerry's lap.

Paulie's anger deflated like a stuck balloon. She was exhausted, confused and scared. Jerry might have been really hurt.

"I want to ride him," Jerry said.

Paulie's voice was weary. "You can't."

"Can, too. He's my horse."

Paulie took hold of her brother's shoulders and stared straight into his eyes. "He's not your horse, Jerry, he's my horse. I put him here and he's not supposed to be here; so we have to keep it a secret."

"Why?"

"Because if anyone finds out he is here, he'll be hauled away and shot and he'll end up on your plate as a piece of horse burger."

"Gross!" Jerry yelled.

"Shhh! So will you keep it a secret?"

Jerry took his time. "I guess so, if you'll let me ride him."

Paulie sighed. "I can't. How about if I let you sit on him?"

"I wanna ride him."

"Sitting or nothing."

"Okay, I'll sit on him."

Paulie lifted him off the bench and put him on Duke's back. Duke shifted his weight and Jerry clutched a handful of mane. "Giddyup," he said, waving his free arm like a rodeo cowboy.

In spite of herself, Paulie thought how her little brother cowboy, with his thick brown curls and his laughing eyes, was really cute. She was amused. "Where do you think you're going?" she asked.

"He's taking me far away to ... to somewhere only I can go."

"Where's that?"

"Never, never land."

"Oh. Are you Peter Pan, then?"

"Yup. This is Tinker Bell's friend and he's taking me someplace Captain Hook won't get me."

She reached up and lifted him down. "Okay, Peter, he's taken you to the enchanted forest. Now it's time for you to go and hide downstairs in your tree house with the other lost boys."

"I don't want to. I want to stay here."

"Well, Duke and I need you to go because some big monsters will be getting up really soon and we don't want them to come out here and find this hideout."

"Can I come back?"

"Maybe later. But you have to promise me you won't come inside the shed again without me."

"But Roger and me are..."

Paulie was out of patience. "Jerry!"

"You never used to be so cranky," he said. He spat on his fingers and crossed his heart. Paulie did not see the hand he held behind his back.

"Thank you. When you go into the house, take your snowsuit off right away. I'll come in in a few minutes and give you some breakfast. And remember, no matter what, you can't say anything about Duke to anyone."

When he was gone, Paulie buried her face in Duke's mane, trying to ease her aching head. She didn't know how Jerry had discovered him, but since he had it would only be a matter of time before someone else did the same, either on their own or because Jerry spilled the beans. She would have to skip school again. She had to get Duke away from here and the hay out of Nana's room today. She patted Duke's neck. With more confidence than she felt she said, "Don't worry, boy, we'll find a place for you."

She moved to the back of the shed to get his breakfast and realized the floor was slick with manure and urine because there was no bedding to keep things dry. If she left it like that, Duke might slip on the wet wood and twist an ankle. But there wasn't time to clean it up now. She fed him two flakes of the hay she'd brought from Nana's and scattered the rest on the floor to help sop up the wet. It would have to do. She'd come back as soon as she'd fed Jerry.

In the small footprints outside the shed there were blotches of brown, but the snow was deep and Jerry's boots were clean before he got to the house. Paulie took a minute to clean off her own boots and to scuff out the offending prints.

Jerry's boots were not on the landing inside the door and there were no wet footprints leading up. She hoped he'd gone downstairs, back to bed.

Her parents were in the kitchen, speaking together in low tones when she walked in. Before she could say anything, the front door of the house opened and her mother called out, "In here, Dorothy." Her grandmother appeared.

"It's hay!" she shrilled. "She's got a ton of hay in there!"

Paulie's father's eyes travelled to his daughter. "Calm down, Mother. I'm sure there's an explanation."

A hand inside Paulie clutched her stomach and squeezed.

Her grandmother's voice broke. "This morning she left me a note saying she'd called a taxi and gone to early services. She'd left the door to her room unlocked; so I looked in and there's hay piled up against an entire wall. Why would anyone put hay in their bedroom? It's crazy behaviour. I never know what she's going to do anymore. She's getting more senile every day."

Hot spots burned in Paulie's cheeks. "Nana's not senile!" she said sharply. "It's my fault. I took the hay to your house, Grandma. All Nana did was keep it for me."

"I didn't do it!" Jerry hollered his way into the house.

Paulie spun and met him as he came up the stairs from the back landing. "Didn't do what?" she demanded.

"I thought you were still there. I only wanted to show Roger my flying saucer. I didn't know it'd make him smash the door and jump the fence."

Paulie was out the door of the house before he finished. She saw the broken door of the shed and the hoofprints leading to the fence. She raced into the alley. The hoofprints were spaced far apart. Duke was running hard. She ran as fast as she could, following them.

— Fifteen —

At seven that night, the family was downstairs in the family room. Jerry was asleep on the couch. Gloria and Sam were lying on the carpet, watching television. Paulie's mother was sitting in a chair, talking on the telephone to her father. "Ed's group has combed the north and west sides of town," he said on his cellphone, "and we've done the south and east. No one's seen any sign of Paulie or the horse so far. Mom and I have been out to the stable. The buildings are still standing, so at least if she does go there there's some shelter. The market garden Paulie talked about has been flattened. I took Mom home. She was done in."

"Shouldn't you come home for something hot to eat?" Paulie's mother said. "You've been out for so long."

"I'm at the truck stop a couple of miles south of town. I'll grab a cup of coffee and soup or something. I want to do one more trip out to the stable, just in case. I'm sure the horse will head back to what he knows."

"It's dark out, Len, and it's forecast for a blizzard."

"I know," he said.

Paulie didn't hear any of that. She closed the back door and went straight up to her room, where she sank onto her pillow. She sat very still even when Perfect came and climbed into her lap.

"Len!" Paulie's mother said to her father. "She's home! I just heard her come in."

"Thank God!" he breathed. "I'll call Ed and ask him to let his group know and I'll notify my guys. Then I'll be home."

"All right." She hung up and sighed. "Gloria, Sammy, come back down here please."

"We were just going to ..." Gloria began.

"I'd like you to stay down here, please. I want to speak with Paulie alone."

They came back down the stairs; Paulie's mother went up.

There was a soft rap on Paulie's bedroom door and her mother came in and sat on her bed. "Paulie," her mother said, "we were so worried about you."

Paulie didn't trust herself to talk. She bit her lip.

Her mother got off the bed and knelt on the floor beside her, sitting back on her heels as Paulie often did. She looked into Paulie's face. "Daddy and Grandma have been out looking for you all day. I'm glad you came home," she said.

"I'm sorry, Mom," Paulie whispered. "I'm sorry for everything."

"Your father and I are sorry, too," her mother said softly. "Did you find Duke?"

Paulie's heart broke. "No," she choked. "I looked for him everywhere, but I couldn't find him. I have to find him. He won't know what to do, where to go. He's all alone out there."

Her mother reached for her and Paulie fell into her warmth. Her body shook with her sobs.

After a time her mother said, "Your father will be home soon."

Paulie pushed herself away. She stared at her gloved hands. Without self-pity she said, "And then? If Daddy finds him, Duke will die. He doesn't care about Duke. He doesn't care about me. All I am to him is trouble."

"Oh, Paulie, that's not true. Your father loves you very much."

Paulie said nothing. Her mother just didn't know.

Her mother reached for one of her hands. Paulie flinched.

"Let me see," her mother said. Gently she pulled off a glove. With infinite care she removed the tape and then the gauze. She fought to keep her voice level when she said, "I think you did a fine job with this. It looks like it will heal. Is the other hand this bad?"

"I don't know," Paulie said.

"We'll clean them up and put on some fresh bandages. Then I think you should have a hot soak in the tub and something hot to eat."

Paulie followed her mother to the bathroom.

Her father did not come home in the hour she spent bathing and eating. Sam and Gloria drank hot cocoa and listened to her story of the past week and of her search for

Duke. Sam wouldn't let her leave anything out. Gloria was astounded to learn what Nana had done at the auction, standing up and challenging the meat buyer like that.

As Paulie told the story, the pain that had filled her stomach, chest and heart and was pulling her neck down into her shoulders loosened. Her body began to relax. But she was not free of care. At the end she said, "I tried to follow his hoofprints. I went everywhere they went, but then he ran onto the road and the cars messed them up. I couldn't see where he'd gone anymore so I went everywhere we'd been, but I couldn't find him." More to herself than to her brother and sister, she whispered, "What if he gets hit by a car?"

"Don't be a dumbbell," Gloria said. "How many cars do you think are driving around in this storm? He'll probably be okay."

Paulie hoped she was right.

Jerry was carried to bed. Grandma called to say she was glad Paulie was safe. They'd deal with the hay situation another day, she said. "You put us through a lot, young lady," she added.

"I know," Paulie said. "I'm sorry."

Her father phoned and told her mother he had slid off the road and was stuck in a snowbank but he was all right. A tow truck would get to him as soon as possible. He thought maybe another hour.

"Paulie," her mother said, "your father won't be home for at least an hour. You can barely hold your head up. Why don't you go on up to bed."

"I can't. I have to look for Duke some more."

Her mother shook her head. "You won't do Duke or yourself any good, the shape you're in, and anyone still out in this storm is taking a real chance. Your father has slid off the road and even if it wasn't a blizzard it's too dark to see anything. You'll have to wait until tomorrow. Please go to bed." Paulie did as she was told, but she did not believe she would get any sleep. Not as long as Duke was out there, somewhere, in the freezing cold. She was wrong. Almost before her head hit the pillow, she was asleep. She woke at five-thirty, waited until six and couldn't stand it any longer. She went to her parents' room. Her father was not there. Her mother was asleep but woke at the sound of Paulie's tread.

"Your father ended up having to spend the night in a truck stop," her mother said. "He should be home soon."

Paulie couldn't wait. Leaving a note for her father to tell him she'd gone to search, she left the house.

The morning lay quiet. In places the snow was knee deep. The going would be tough. She went to the shed and got her skis from the rafters. Many times in the past two winters she had skied to the stable.

Duke still wasn't at his old barn or at any of the farms south of the city. He wasn't in any of the city parks, either, and she hadn't seen him on any of the side streets she'd travelled. She went to the newspaper office, where she put an advertisement in the paper, describing Duke the best way she could. She included her name and phone number.

The clerk suggested she call a local radio station and put out the alert. She helped Paulie do that.

The SPCA — otherwise known to Paulie as the dog-catcher — only kept dogs and cats, but they might know about a loose horse, she thought. She went there. A slender girl with bright red hair smiled at her. "Hello. Are you looking for a kitten or a puppy? There aren't many kittens this time of year, but we have a wonderful new batch of puppies. They look like a lab cross."

"No," Paulie said. "I'm looking for my horse. He ran away."

"We don't keep horses here," the girl said.

"I know, but I thought maybe your dogcatchers might have seen him or ..."

"I don't think so," the girl said. "At least there hasn't been any report from anyone saying they've seen a horse. But I can take a description and pass it on to our drivers."

"All right."

The girl took out a form and picked up a pen. "When did your horse go missing?" she asked.

"Yesterday."

"What area was it in?"

"The southeast end of town."

"Can you describe him?"

"He's a grey with a white mane and tail. He's fifteen-three hands high. He looks like a quarter horse, but he runs like a thoroughbred," Paulie said.

The girl smiled.

Paulie hesitated, not wanting to tell the next part because it embarrassed her, but she knew it set Duke apart. "His forelock has been cut like bangs," she said and added quickly, "and he's wearing a blue halter with a braided binder-twine rope attached to it."

"I'll put it on the radio," the girl said. "All our van drivers will keep their eyes open."

Paulie thanked her.

The only other place Paulie could think to look was the auction. Duke knew his way there and runaway horses usually went back to someplace they knew. She headed back out of town.

Duke wasn't in any of the outside pens. In the arena a pile of goods had been amassed in the centre of the sales ring for Sunday's sale, but there were no people in the ring, the auctioneers' booth or the stands. In the hallway to the office Paulie met a man she had seen before. He was wearing the same red plaid jacket.

"You were here last Sunday," she said.

He looked down at her.

"You bid against me for a grey horse named Duke. I bought him."

"Could be," he said.

"Can you tell me if he came back here?"

"That would be one of the fastest turnarounds in history," the man chuckled.

"No, I mean, he wouldn't be here to be sold again. He ... ran away yesterday and I thought maybe he might have come back here."

"I wasn't here yesterday," the man said. "Ain't seen him today. Check at the office."

Paulie went to the office. A man she didn't recognize was sitting on a desk with his leg propped over one corner. He was holding a batch of papers, reading the top page. "Excuse me," she said, "could you tell me if a grey horse wearing a blue halter with a binder-twine rope attached came here yesterday or today? His name's Duke."

"The old foot stomper," the man said knowingly.

"That's him!"

"He was wandering around the horse pens yesterday afternoon. The boss put him in one."

Paulie's face lit up. "You've got him!"

"Nope. He was picked up this mornin'."

For Paulie the room seemed to tilt. "How could he be picked up if he's my horse?" she asked weakly.

"You got proof?"

Anger replaced her dizziness. "Yes."

He waited, swinging a foot.

"My bill of sale is at home," she said. "But I bought him here. You have to have a record of it."

The man glanced at the filing cabinet, but didn't move. "Well now, I suppose there is a record, all right. Trouble is, it won't help 'cause the horse isn't here."

"Don't you keep the names of people you give other people's horses to?" she snapped.

"Well, now, I'd suppose we'd gen'ally make sure the

people we're givin' 'em to owns 'em and we check the fees have been paid if there are any. But in this case the boss released the horse. He knew the fella personally."

"Don't you know who it was?"

"Sorry, I just started working here."

"Then can I please ask the boss?"

"Sure. Come back in about two weeks. That's when he'll be back from his buyin' trip."

Paulie felt empty — hollow. Her words echoed inside her head like someone calling down a long tin tube. "Did he … did Duke get taken by Railway Three?" she asked. "You have to tell me."

The man had no more time for her. "I told you, you'll have to ask the boss. Now I've got a lotta work to do, kid, and not a whole lot of time to do it, so you're gonna have to leave." He ushered her to the door and closed it firmly behind her.

She stood with her shoulder against a wall, gasping back her tears. The world went blurry. There was nowhere else to go. She went outside, put her skis on and went home.

Gloria was in the kitchen. "Dad's in the living room waiting for you," she said when Paulie came in. Paulie didn't answer. "Grandma and Nana are here, too, and there's someone else."

Paulie sighed. *Here it comes*, she thought. *More trouble.* She went to the living room. At the arched doorway, she stopped. Of all the people on this earth, Bob was the last person she wanted to see right now. And there he was, sitting in her mother's chair, smiling at her. Paulie wanted to run. Instead, she stared at the carpet.

"I believe I may have something that belongs to you," Bob said. "He's fat and he's sassy."

Slowly Bob's words sank in. "You!" she yelled. "You're the one who got Duke from the auction!"

"Yup. I was delivering the trailer when I spotted him. Wearin' his halter and rope like that I figured you'd temporarily misplaced him and I didn't think you needed a board bill from those fellas, so I talked old Buzz into letting me take him. Didn't take much talking. Buzz left on his buyin' trip with one mighty sore big toe."

Paulie ran to the front window. "You've got him here?"

"Right out there in that trailer. Where would you like me to put him?"

Paulie looked at each of the adults. As fast as it had flared, her hope vanished. It was over. She looked at the floor and wound her fingers in knots. She couldn't bring herself to say it, but she had to. "I can't take good care of him. I can't keep him. He has to go back to the auction," she said.

Bob's rough voice sounded unusually soft. "Do you want to ride in the trailer with him?"

"No. Thank you."

With that, she turned and left the room. Outside, in the shed, she cried until she thought she had no tears left.

— Sixteen —

Saturday afternoon, Jenny showed up at the house. "I brought notes and home-work for Paulie," she said when Paulie's mother opened the door. "I thought maybe she was sick." Paulie's mother sent her upstairs.

Paulie told Jenny the whole story. She had thought she was cried out, but in the telling she cried again, and Jenny's eyes watered too. No scold of any kind came. In the cama-raderie of shared sorrow the two friends' differences were forgotten, and they spent a blue afternoon in happy company.

After supper, Jenny suggested they go to a movie. *Hot Chick* was still playing, and Jenny would watch it again. It was hilarious, she told Paulie. But Paulie didn't really find it very funny.

The following day Paulie went to the auction. Last night she had been determined she wasn't going to go, but this morning she knew she would. She had to say a proper goodbye.

She'd spent the early morning cleaning up the hay bits that had been left in Nana's room when Bob carried it back to the trailer to take it away. Nana had helped with the cleaning. Before they'd finished, Grandma had come to the doorway. "I do love the brightness of this room, Dorothy," Nana said.

"I know, Mom," Grandma said, "and there's room for all your things here and it's flat. No stairs. I think maybe I've been wrong. You're right to want to stay."

Nana beamed and said simply, "Thank you, dear."

Paulie had offered to help bring Nana's things back. Grandma was surprisingly strong. It hadn't taken long.

There were just some things you wanted to do alone. Paulie had wanted to come to the auction by herself, but her father had insisted on driving her and Nana said she would like to come if Paulie didn't mind, and Paulie could not say no, and then Jenny had shown up. So here they were, the crowd of them, standing outside the paddock where Duke was. Exactly one week had passed since she had bought Duke. One short week that had seemed to Paulie to be at least a whole year long.

The others stood outside the fence while she climbed through the rails. She went to her horse and put her arms around his neck. "I'll always remember you, boy," she said. "I love you." She could not stop her tears from flowing again.

Then her father was beside her, rubbing Duke's poll, stroking his ear. "He's a good old fellow," her father said. He put an arm on Paulie's shoulders. "I wish we could keep him, Paulie, with all my heart I wish we could," and Paulie sank backwards into him, feeling a warming comfort she hadn't felt for a long time.

"I hear you're sellin' that horse," a man said behind them.

Paulie jumped. Dropping her arms from Duke's neck, she rubbed her eyes, straightening her shoulders unconsciously. She did not turn around. "Yes," she said.

"Well, I want to buy him an' I'd just as soon not go through the auction to get him," the man said. "Price o' meat's too damn high. One of those other suckers'll likely outbid me. He ain't worth what I'd have to pay for him then unless I let him go for meat."

Paulie turned. It was the man from Railway Three. Beside him stood the boy Paulie had thought belonged with the man in the red plaid jacket.

"I want him for my boy," the meat buyer said.

The boy darted into the pen and came close to the horse. "Can I get on him?" he asked.

Paulie leaned down to give him a leg up.

"I can do it," the boy said. He backed up and ran toward the horse. As he leaped, Duke sidestepped out of his reach. The youngster hit the ground. He came up sputtering — mad, not hurt.

Paulie laughed out loud.

"It isn't funny," the little boy growled.

"It is," Paulie said, "but don't worry, you can learn to outsmart him. Want a leg up now?"

The boy put his foot into her cupped hands and she lifted him onto Duke's back. Duke looked as if he was asleep.

"I'll pay you what you paid for him, plus I'll pay the auction commission they'll charge you for registerin' him and not selling him," the man said. "If you want to talk it over with your father, I'll be around here all day and most of the night."

She didn't have to talk it over or think about it at all. "It's okay," she said. "You can have him."

"I know where you can get some hay to go with that horse," Bob said. "Cheap. Eighty-five bucks a ton."

The meat buyer grinned. "You old shyster. Where'd you come from? Don't think I don't know you probably got it for half that price."

"Would I do that to a friend?" Bob asked.

"You would."

"Yup," Bob allowed, "I would. But if you don't buy it from me at eighty-five, you'll pay a hundred elsewhere. Case you haven't heard, it was a bad year for hay."

Paulie and her father climbed out of the pen. Paulie's father asked Bob if he'd like to come to the house for lunch after he'd finished his business here. Bob said that would be mighty fine.

In the car, her father and Nana rode in the front. Paulie and Jenny were in the back.

Her father shook his head. "Being here brings back memories. I almost miss this kind of thing."

"Me, too," Nana said. "My family called me horse crazy when I was a girl and I said the same thing to Dorothy when she was a girl."

"That makes three," Paulie's father said. "She said the same to me."

"Well, Dad ..." Paulie said, and everyone laughed.

"Now," her father said, "we'll talk about the two Saturdays of cleaning you're going to do at the church to make restitution for a certain unwanted load your horse left there."

"We will?" Paulie said.

"Yes," her father said.

"Yes," Paulie sighed, "I guess we will."

— Acknowledgements —

Emily Mascal read the very first draft of this book when she was twelve, and cried. It gave me all the oomph I needed to keep going with it. Stephanie Christensen, Bill Reekie, Carol MacRae, Heather Kellerhals, Jeanette Taylor, Annette Yourk and Ian Douglas provided encouragement, assistance, and loving support along the way. Rowan and Garnet Kehn and Murray Garland's grade five/six class at Quadra Elementary School took time to vote on titles. Lynn Henry did the editing with a gentle hand and it's her title on the cover and the spine. Julia Bell worked her magic for the cover painting. Warmest thanks to all of you.

— About the Author —

Jocelyn Reekie is the author of the acclaimed historical novel *Tess* (Raincoast, 2002), about a thirteen-year-old girl named Tess Macqueen who sails from Scotland to British Columbia in 1857. Jocelyn lives on Quadra Island, British Columbia, where she shares her life with her husband and two children, and a variety of animals — including horses. She is hard at work on a sequel to *Tess*.